FLAWED ANGEL

John Fuller is an acclaimed novelist and poet. His novel *Flying to Nowhere* was shortlisted for the Booker Prize; *Stones and Fires* won the Forward Poetry Prize in 1996, and his latest collection, *Ghosts*, was shortlisted for the Whitbread Poetry Prize in 2004. He is an Emeritus Fellow of Magdalen College, Oxford.

ALSO BY JOHN FULLER

Fiction

Flying to Nowhere
The Adventures of Speedfall
Tell It Me Again
The Burning Boys
Look Twice
The Worm and the Star
A Skin Diary
*The Memoirs of Laetitia
Horsepole*

Poetry

Fairground Music
The Tree that Walked
Cannibals and Missionaries
Epistles to Several Persons
The Mountain in the Sea
Lies and Secrets
The Illusionists
Waiting for the Music
The Beautiful Inventions
Selected Poems 1954 to 1982
Partingtime Hall
(with James Fenton)
The Grey Among the Green
The Mechanical Body
Stones and Fires
Collected Poems
Now and for a Time
Ghosts
The Space of Joy

Criticism

The Sonnet
W.H. Auden: a Commentary

For Children

Herod Do Your Worst
Squeaking Crust
The Spider Monkey Uncle King
The Last Bid
*The Extraordinary Wool
Mill and Other Stories*
Come Aboard and Sail Away

Edited

*The Chatto Book
of Love Poetry*
*The Dramatic Works
of John Gay*
The Oxford Book of Sonnets
*W.H. Auden: Poems Selected
by John Fuller*

JOHN FULLER

Flawed Angel

A Tale

WITHDRAWN

VINTAGE BOOKS
London

Published by Vintage 2006

2 4 6 8 10 9 7 5 3 1

Copyright © John Fuller 2005

John Fuller has asserted his right under the Copyright,
Designs and Patents Act, 1988 to be identified as the author
of this work

First published in Great Britain in 2005 by
Chatto & Windus

Vintage
Random House, 20 Vauxhall Bridge Road,
London SW1V 2SA

Random House Australia (Pty) Limited
20 Alfred Street, Milsons Point, Sydney,
New South Wales 2061, Australia

Random House New Zealand Limited
18 Poland Road, Glenfield, Auckland 10, New Zealand

Random House (Pty) Limited
Isle of Houghton, Corner of Boundary Road & Carse O'Gowrie,
Houghton, 2198, South Africa

Random House Publishers India Private Limited
301 World Trade Tower, Hotel Intercontinental Grand Complex,
Barakhamba Lane, New Delhi 110 001, India

The Random House Group Limited Reg. No. 954009
www.randomhouse.co.uk/vintage

A CIP catalogue record for this book
is available from the British Library

ISBN 9780099488927 (from Jan 2007)
ISBN 0099488922

Papers used by Random House are natural,
recyclable products made from wood grown in
sustainable forests. The manufacturing processes
conform to the environmental regulations of the
country of origin

Printed and bound in Great Britain by
Bookmarque Ltd, Croydon, Surrey

Even the shortest life is partitioned out by some people into four; by others into six, and by others again into a still larger number of periods; that is to say, the reality is so small, and as you cannot make it larger, you think you will enlarge it by division. But of what profit is all this dividing? Make as many particles as you like, and they are all gone in a moment, in the twinkling of an eye.

Petrarch, *Secretum*, Dialogue the Third

1

'YOUR Exaltedness, he is alive!'

The ragged man came recklessly out of the crowd, smiling a foolish smile of good will, and approached Juliba's swaying litter.

The footmen were astonished, and looked for a guard to take the man away. But having almost reached the foot of the palace steps, the guards had already deployed themselves in ceremonial rank. They were too far away to act, intent on facing inwards to receive the procession, thrusting out their chests and staring straight ahead in front of them.

Kites circled high in the sky, as though inscribing sentences of tribute upon invisible domes. A dog barked.

The man came nearer, putting out his hand. The crowd collectively drew in its breath, as at the climax of the birthday fireworks, or when Dibl seized the headless goat over his shoulder and galloped with it the full length of the field. Those too far away to see his idiot smile thought he was an assassin. Those near enough to hear him were curious about his words.

Juliba turned to face him from the litter, and her eyes looked down over her veil superb as the two towers on the dam at Sarapa which keeps back the full power of the spring waters.

'He is alive! Be assured!' the man repeated. And in his eagerness to bring such news and to be believed, his fingers for a moment touched the queen's arm as it rested on the door of the litter.

Now the crowd groaned, fearing the outcome of this scandalous contact.

Juliba looked about her.

'Surely it is apparent', she said, 'that I do not need the blessings of a beggar?'

The footmen had put the litter down. In her haste to leave it and to mount the palace steps, her robes twisted about her as she stood up and defined for a moment the fullness of her belly. The footmen themselves took hold of the man, who was grinning and nodding vigorously, and handed him over to the guards, amid the press of the wondering crowd.

And Juliba mounted the steps with dignity, and entered the palace with her attendants, and the doors of her apartments were closed upon her.

The man was brought before the ruling Akond,

in-Blemim, who was troubled when he heard what had happened.

'How is it', he thought, 'that our actions cannot be perfectly controlled? That however well-intended, they return to haunt us with their unforeseen consequences? That sometimes the good intended by others is the very worst thing that we wish to hear?'

He took the ragged man to be a creature of his Wazir, Ininin, come to trade secrets for favours. Alive, was it, when ordered destroyed? Well, then, Ininin should deal with the matter, and silence this madman.

And so the Akond ordered the man, who was a carpenter named 'm Ezla, to be taken to the Wazir's court for judgement.

'How can it be tolerated', he thought to himself, 'that a carpenter, touching the least hem of my wife's robe, should pronounce the blessing of life where there is none? Neither in the born who are dead, nor in the unborn who are not yet alive? Why, it is a Christian nonsense, and the people will see it to be so.'

The Akond went in to Juliba, his queen, and was relieved to find that it was so with her, and he put his own hand freely on the shape that would be his heir, measuring the child's vigour in protesting at further confinement by comparing his kicks to those motions necessary to goad the girth of a great horse into a gallop. He was disappointed to find them sluggish.

But he smiled at Juliba in encouragement, his teeth showing white within the majesty of his black beard and his eyes gleaming like polished agate.

The crowd had not dispersed, and it was not thought likely that it would disperse until the fate of 'm Ezla was announced. It moved in the square like bees over the comb, sharing opinion until it might take the perfect sweetness and structure of fact.

The Wazir Ininin was seated with his officials behind a marble table. Not his beard, nor his small derisive mouth struck fear into those who were brought before him, but his immense nose that jutted above those features like the beak of an eagle. It was a symbol of his power to probe and rend.

But the Wazir's heart sank when 'm Ezla came before him, for he knew him to be the brother of the wife of Bagril, his agent in the villages, and knew him, too, as a fool who might wittingly or unwittingly unravel any delicate scheme with no profit to himself or any sensible forethought of the outcome. So foolish, in fact, as to be quite without the necessary fear of civilised men.

'You touched the queen's arm?' asked the Wazir Ininin.

'Excellence, the child –' began 'm Ezla, with the eagerness of someone who knows himself to be almost dignified by the possession of astounding news.

'Enough,' said Ininin. 'We do not wish to hear of it.'

'But, Excellence, it is a miracle!'

'Do you want to lose more than your fingers?' thundered the Wazir. 'There is nothing that you can tell me that I can possibly want to hear. You touched the queen on the arm with two fingers, with three? The forefinger and the middle finger, I hear? And perhaps also the fourth finger?'

Witnesses were produced among the Akond's servants to swear to the lesser of these charges. One of the footmen, indeed, was of the opinion that perhaps only the middle finger had grazed the queen's arm, had been in contact for an instant only with the fold of her cloak, even. But this opinion belonged to the minority, and accordingly the carpenter was sentenced.

'm Ezla seemed unconcerned about his punishment, and when later that afternoon he was led before the executioner he made no protest except to reiterate his proclamation of a miracle: 'The child lives!' For this, and to preserve the silence and gravity of the occasion, a scarf was bound about his mouth and he appeared dumb before the crowd in the courtyard.

The executioner, whom the pain of his vocation had turned into a wag, seized 'm Ezla's hand, extending the offending fingers and folding back the rest in a parody of the blessing that Juliba had spurned, and exhibited it on high to the crowd, who laughed and groaned in equal measure. Then he pressed the hand down upon the ebony block with the two fingers extended, and raised his short axe.

The Akond was watching from a high window of the palace, unseen: 'In the necessary chain of command there are many weak links,' he said to himself. 'They must be cut out, so that the pull may be secure.'

The axe descended, and in the hush of the crowd you might almost have heard the tiny doubleness of the blow, the cadence between bone and wood, as the blade finally met the substance that could resist it, and the severed fingers shot across the polished surface and fell into the dust.

'He will speak of it no more,' thought the Akond.

'But if the child really lives, it is grotesque, and cannot be allowed.'

And Juliba in her apartments, with her heart pounding, knew that the incident had really given her no grounds to raise the matter again, for whatever was done was done for the best. Whatever her attendants did, they did it for her good and for the good of the country. They did what was expected.

When she had first come to the palace and danced for in-Blemim, she had had vague hopes of finding good reason for a woman to play a meaningful role in the affairs of state, not least in alleviating the conditions of the poor. And she confessed as much to uz-Luba, in-Blemim's grandmother, expecting to discover somewhere within the law some such licence for a queen.

'Yes, my beautiful,' uz-Luba had smiled at her. 'So you think, and so have we all thought at this threshold of our life and fortune. And you being both a woman and knowing poverty have a double reason to hope for a rational justice. And for in-Blemim, too, who lives by reason, you have a right to suppose an equal desire. But the Akond rules only through the people and by custom. To live by custom is to live by expectation; laws are generally resented.'

'And if custom does not bring justice to all?'

'Custom should be the happiness of all, as being what can least be resented.'

And uz-Luba had nodded at this with such quiet certainty that Juliba had created no further argument, but hung her arms about her neck and embraced her.

During the night after 'm Ezla lost his fingers, the queen's waters broke and she was delivered of her sluggish son. It was natural after this to forget the incident in front of the palace steps, but occasionally in dreams the carpenter's face would appear to her, eager, shining, complicit, communicating a fact that she had steeled herself to deny.

When the Akond had inspected his heir, he went in to congratulate Juliba.

'Blom is perfect,' he said. 'He has eyes like honey and skin as pale as olives. And he has just the right number of toes – and fingers.'

Juliba and in-Blemim looked at each other with that look of intimate wedded conspiracy which can sometimes exclude a truth. He lolled at her feet, eating dates and reciting lines of poetry that suddenly occurred to him in his happiness, though occasionally he would grimace in pain, for the dates brought on his toothache:

'When the streams of Sarapa meet in the valley,
When the streams of Sarapa brim in the spring,
Hearts must melt in the fullness of water
Thudding like swimmers to whose weary shoulders
          The waters cling.

The furthest echo was once a spent volley.
The furthest echo was once a false start
Where the heart was launched in its lightness of
    being,
Shot from desire like the swimmer for whom
          The waters part.

The little swimmer, in his perfect prison!
The little swimmer in the borrowed skin
That bares the heart like the blueness of snow
In the beautiful mountains above Sarapa where
          The waters begin!'

   This tenderness for the child brought him to a
deep and unqualified joy, and he laughed aloud.
   The carpenter's fingers were eaten by the dogs.

2

SOON after the birth of Blom, in-Blemim took it upon himself to inform his own father, uz-Blemim, in person. He took three of his best horses, and rode for three days to the spice fields at Samira, leaving the ridden horses at villages on the way to recover in time for his return journey.

The old Akond received the news with a mixture of joy and resignation, pouring wine as though it weighed in the jar like oil.

'A new life is a blessed event,' he said. 'But we cannot help regarding it with terror.'

The Akond heard his father in amazement.

'Terror?' he said. 'What can you mean? The new life secures the future of our family and the happiness of the country.'

They took their beakers of wine, and drank.

'The happiness of the country?' said the older man. 'I can understand the happiness of individuals, but a country can be neither happy nor unhappy. At any time, some people will be happy and some will be unhappy. What more can be said?'

They sat on a paved terrace in the cool of the evening, as father and son may do, looking out over the spice fields. The Akond did not understand his father.

'What are you terrified about?' he asked. 'Where is the terror in the birth of your grandson?'

'I felt it last year, with the prospect of your first-born,' said uz-Blemim. 'But I said nothing of it, and the child's death put it from me. Now the life of this new son more certainly tells me that I shall die.'

In-Blemim touched his father briefly on the sleeve.

'You are very far from death,' he said, firmly.

'How far?' asked uz-Blemim.

'How far?' echoed in-Blemim. 'You are not ill, I trust? Are you hiding something from me?'

'Nothing,' said uz-Blemim. 'I am sound enough.'

He flicked his beaker with a finger-nail, and its note rang out in the still evening air.

In-Blemim laughed, but nervously. To hide his uncertainty about his father's state of mind, he flicked his own beaker, and a different note rang out. His father smiled and responded, and the little cadence tinkled for a time from the terrace like a prayer-bell.

'In full health, I assure you,' said uz-Blemim. 'The mountain air is, as you see, fresh and invigorating, and it encourages long life. The under-manager of the plantations has a great-great-grandfather who is 110 years old.'

'Through living on air?' suggested in-Blemim, with a smile.

'The diet here is simple,' said the old Akond. 'And the work is hard. But I also believe that there is great benefit to be gained from the drying of the spice harvest. I sometimes go into the sheds just before the baling, and I sit and breathe in the aroma. The particles of the spice are everywhere in the air. You can see them in the shafts of sunlight that slant in from the high windows. Even when the harvest has been baled and is on its way down the river, the scent remains. Can you not smell it now, even from here?'

The Akond acknowledged that he could indeed faintly smell the spice.

'Perhaps then,' he said, 'you will live to be 110 yourself. Or more?'

'That is neither here nor there,' replied uz-Blemim. 'There are stages towards death, and there is relative lightness of heart until the next stage is reached. The death of my father was one stage. The birth of your son is another. There is no turning back. Now I must measure my life in terms of the Three Gifts.'

Then they were both silent for a while, thinking about this. The old Akond refilled their beakers with wine.

The Three Gifts to which he had referred marked three stages in the coming of age of each successive Akond. They were symbols of maturity and power, but they were also actual gifts, tangibly bestowed. The first, given to the heir at the age of seven, was a white horse, conventionally the finest miniature horse that could be found. It represented the end of childhood and the beginning of that self-control and control of others that belonged to warriorhood. The second, given when he reached fourteen, was a beautiful bride, conventionally the fairest virgin that could be found. She represented the beginning of adulthood and the eventual generation of future Akonds. The third, given at the age of twenty-one, was a golden key to the coffers of the palace. This represented a transference of power. Henceforward the young Akond became the Akond, and took upon himself the rule of the kingdom. His bride was now permitted to conceive a child. The Akond became the old Akond, and retired to manage the spice fields.

'You see,' said uz-Blemim, 'that in the space of thrice seven years you will replace me here, and I must die.'

'It will not happen like that, of course,' said in-Blemim.

'Only in the sense that death itself is unpredictable,' replied uz-Blemim. 'But the idea is there. It seems to me to be a part of the tradition.'

'Well,' said in-Blemim, 'you will have no reason to die. You will have to find some other occupation.'

'Keeper of wheeled chairs and warming-pans, do you mean?'

'Enough of this,' said in-Blemim.

'Yes, yes, you are right,' said his father. 'I have enough to keep myself occupied. But do not imagine that the twenty-one years will seem like anything much. The Three Gifts will pass as fleetingly as the three days you have spent in getting here, and the years themselves are nothing save what may be recorded in them. And what is beyond them? The pattern repeats itself, as new blood is required. The old blood is cast aside. As the poet has truly written:

A Tale

"The years that go, where are they going?
We who remember pause and say
The years have passed beyond our knowing.

At first, upon the brink of growing,
Thoughtless we spent the endless day.
The years that go, where are they going?

Oh, what we waste with nothing owing
And only happy hours of play!
The years have passed beyond our knowing.

And life is hastening, not slowing.
The mountain waters run away.
The years that go, where are they going?

The rice is ignorant of sowing,
The rain unconscious of delay.
The years have passed beyond our knowing.

And we are of the world that's flowing,
Powerless to make it stay.
The years that go, where are they going?
The years have passed beyond our knowing.'"

And the old Akond sighed deeply. He watched a
green spice-beetle crawl along the chequered tiles of

the terrace, and reflected that, when it had finished labouring across its terracotta tile and was crossing over to the safety of a turquoise one, he could lift his foot and crush it. Or he could allow it to cross the turquoise tile and wait until it reached another terracotta one. Or he could spare it altogether, as he was inclined to do, for one of his oldest house-servants was a Jain, and he respected the man's tenderness for all creatures. 'My intentions are unknown to the beetle,' he thought, 'and yet the beetle is content. It makes a strange colour on the turquoise, which pleases me. But the beetle knows nothing of that, either. Truly, it is as well that we know little.'

After dinner they walked through the plantations to the dwellings of the workers, to prove their happiness.

In the first hovel they came to, a family was squatting on the floor, gnawing bones. The Akond was shocked. There seemed to be very little meat on the bones, and the younger members of the family were turning them over in their hands or spinning them on the dried mud of the floor rather than eating them.

Are these food or toys, he wondered?

He took his father's arm in embarrassment, as if to say that they should leave, but uz-Blemim stood in the centre of the meagre room, beaming at the worker and his family.

'The Akond is visiting me with news of the birth of his heir. We have come to see if you are contented with your life.'

'Contented, Exaltedness?' exclaimed the worker, bowing his forehead first to the slippers of the Akond and then to the slippers of the old Akond. 'Oh, it is so impossible to measure our contentedness. We are forever in your debt.'

In-Blemim could hardly bear to look at the man as he spoke, but let his eyes stray over the room, in one dark corner of which he could see a girl on a heap of rags who was baring one breast before him, slily, with two fingers.

'Supremely in your debt, Exaltedness,' the man continued to mutter. 'Supremely happy.'

The smell was intolerable.

Afterwards, when they regained the spice-laden air of the fields, in-Blemim turned to his father.

'Do all the workers live like that?' he asked.

Uz-Blemim considered for a moment.

'It is true that I deliberately took you to a family

who live in somewhat more favourable and well-appointed circumstances than most, but you will understand why I wished you to receive a good impression. You will have to forgive me for that.'

'But, Father,' said in-Blemim, 'did you not see their sores?'

'Irritation from the husks of the spice, I'm afraid,' said the old Akond. 'The sores sometimes nearly heal, but then it is always time for the next gathering and they break open again.'

'Is this kind of life bearable?'

'It is life, the most precious gift of all, and under my protection.'

'Do they never seek to end it?'

The old Akond was surprised at this suggestion.

'Do you want me to take you to the hovels of the poorer workers, the feckless and incompetent ones, the lazy, the rebellious, the unclean?' he asked, impatiently. 'I can do so, if it is sores that you want to see.'

'There are worse sores than these?' asked in-Blemim.

'Yes,' said uz-Blemim.

They were silent for a moment.

'The great-great-grandfather of the under-manager

whom you mentioned,' said in-Blemim at last. 'The one who is 110 years old?'

'The worst of all,' said the old Akond, quietly. 'The worst I have ever seen.'

'I do not understand,' replied his son, how you can believe them to be happy, and yet to be without secure happiness yourself.'

And the following day he mounted his horse and left Samira at a gallop.

3

THE AKOND resolved to visit uz-Blemim again only on the significant occasions of the Three Gifts. He found his father's melancholy and self-obsession insufferable.

'He is illogical and deluded,' he said to himself. 'It is as well that he must remain in exile at Samira, even though it is likely that it is exile that has turned his head.'

He also resolved to double the consignment of gold sent to Samira at the time of the spice harvests, with instructions that the workers were to be better housed and fed. But he had no doubt that his father would spend much of this money on himself, on wine and debaucheries, and on liveries for his servants.

The Akond watched his heir grow from a fat baby, blinking and gasping in the arms of his nurse, to an even fatter one lying ceremoniously on his rust-and-ochre carpets.

'Why will he not turn over?' was his frequent question to Juliba. Juliba, who was pleased enough to have a living child and treated him like an ingenious mechanical toy, had no answer to this and did not much care. She would brush the baby's curled knuckles with her forefinger, or insert it into his folded palm, but the little chubby hand showed no inclination to grasp. Blom sighed, and reserved his energy for sucking.

The Akond's younger brother, Anic, the boy's uncle, observed sourly that the child would need more energy if he was ever to govern the country. His own children, fathered on various women of the palace, already ran about shrieking in the inner courtyards, chasing bladders into the fountains or flying kites which became entangled in the balconies. The Akond was irritated by them, as evidence of his brother's indiscriminate pleasures, but, now that he had an heir himself, had no need to fear his brother or any of the sprats that might fall from his loins. Anic had been rutting since the age of twelve, and boasting of his fecundity, but his only real ambition was to challenge the great Dibl on the Field of the Goat, and he was often heard singing the Song of the Goat:

'It has no head to tell it where to go.
The goat is puzzled and the goat is slow.
Once fleet, now meat it lies
And all that once its eyes
Drank from the landscape now it does not know.
Its days of consciousness are fled.
The miles beneath its feet are dead.
To make it stir and rise
It must become a prize.
And now it's moving, very fast, although
It has no head to tell it where to go.'

In the course of time, the child Blom did the things that were expected of him. He became curious about the tiger shapes in his carpets, and turned to look at them. Then he was aware that his rattle lay on the carpets, a little beyond his reach. Once on his stomach, he became aware of his elbows. Once on his elbows, he found that he could raise his head, which he did wearily, without real curiosity. Horizons never lured him, but if something particularly rewarding were put directly into his hand, he would look upon it benignly and even slowly turn it over in case there were some part of it that could be eaten.

Anic's children would put him in their little cart

and pull him in mock-procession down the open corridors of the palace, together with an attendance of stick puppets and a cage of doves. Juliba was content to see him so pampered. It seemed fitting that the young Akond should be prepared for the rituals of adulation.

But Blom could now walk and run, and his playmates fully expected to be pulled in their turn. They were disappointed. He walked only to satisfy some eventually unignorable urge, and ran only to follow. He watched the other children as if to satisfy himself that play was possible, to examine its procedures, and, eventually, to take an aesthetic delight in it. He shared in play like the politest of guests.

His nurse, sponging down the stout expanse of his little belly, allowed a full trickle of water to fall against the prawn of his manhood, as nurses do, expecting him to laugh or to pull at it and show her its future promise. But his responding gaze at her, his moon face lifted to hers as if in rebuke at the unfairness of her demand, almost made her feel ashamed, conscious for the first time of a dignity in impotence.

'Why does he never shout?' thought the Akond to himself. 'Surely children must shout? There are times when he frightens me. He seems almost as rational as I am.'

When the time came near for the celebration of the future Akond's seventh birthday, in-Blemim gave instructions to his Wazir Ininin to procure the finest white horse that could be found, suitable for Blom to ride. Accordingly Ininin sent for his agent Bagril to go into the villages to search the stables of the wealthier farmers, or of anyone who might out of ostentation or fashion keep a horse unsullied by field work. He also consulted with Arab merchants at the port of Taflat, for they were so eager for his country's spice that they were usually willing to provide anything that the Akond desired: Venetian glass, musical boxes, paintings in gilded frames, carriage clocks, any luxury from the West that would impress a visiting Maharajah. Equally, the traders from Goa or Kerala were able to offer tea, silks, ivory or peacocks.

'As always,' the Akond would say to his guests, 'we have the best of both worlds. You may wonder why this spice grows only on our own mountain slopes. You may even think of attempting to cultivate it yourselves. And you surely cannot understand why it is so expensive. Try to grow it! We will even give you cuttings. Then you will have your answers.'

The poet had celebrated the famous spice many times in his verses, not least in his paean to the variety of the world as it appears to the infant:

'What is that scent?
It rises in the air.
Catch it on the skin,
The oils of the hair!

The spice of Samira
On cool evenings,
Crop of the country,
Perfume of kings.

O world inhaled,
Empire of the nose:
Vapour of the grape,
Eucalyptus, rose!

The chemic presence,
Crust and yeast,
Spores of the cellar,
Glow of the feast.

Signal of the flower,
Burning of the leaf:

The scent of joy,
The stench of grief

The world in its heat,
In life, in death:
All the strange smells
Of our first breath.'

The Akond knew that the world could not exist for a day with any relish at all without the use of his spice. To keep in his favour, the Arabs would search for steeds of the purest blood and colour in their desert lands where the horse itself was prince.

As he had promised, in-Blemim then took the three-day journey again to the spice fields to visit his father, the old Akond. He had the idea that his father might be persuaded to return with him to meet Blom and to join in the celebration of the First Gift. Such a visit might cheer him up by showing him that his life could never be over so long as he could share it with his grandson.

'No,' said uz-Blemim. 'It is against tradition. I cannot come. I must make sure of the efficient harvesting of the spice.'

'But for a month or two, surely all will be safe in

the hands of the manager?' protested the Akond, secretly relieved at his father's refusal.

'The manager is dead,' replied uz-Blemim. 'And I have given his position to the under-manager.'

'Well, then?' said in-Blemim.

'A great mistake,' said uz-Blemim. 'The under-manager's father is ill through looking after his great-grandfather, and now the grandfather is dying. He copes with the work of the plantations, but is too preoccupied to take initiatives.'

'Are there no women in this family?' asked in-Blemim.

'All visionaries,' said his father. 'They have joined a mountain cult, and spend all their time chanting together.'

'Is there no one else who could manage the plantations?'

'Yes,' said uz-Blemim decisively. 'I can manage them myself. Which is what I am doing.'

'And are you any more contented?'

'You ask this question of a man who, since you last spoke with him, has consumed one-third of his remaining portion of life?'

'That was not in my mind when I asked the question,' said the Akond, his exasperation none the less tempered by the concern he felt for his father. 'But since you insist upon retaining this artificial boundary to your existence, why don't you look upon it this way: you may have spent a third of your remaining life, as you put it, but you have two-thirds left. Which is twice as much.'

The old Akond stared at him, then tilted back his head and laughed.

'I always knew that you were a philosopher,' he said. 'As a child you argued with your elders, even to the extent of leaving sweetmeats untasted on your plate if the conversation became at all heated. Do you remember?'

The Akond pondered. All he could think was that he very much liked sweetmeats, and did not see why it should not always have been so. But, yes, he was a philosopher.

'Yes, I remember,' he said.

'Now then, I have a present for Blom,' said uz-Blemim.

'Sweetmeats?'

'No, it is this.'

And his father gave him a carved box inside which was a shell. Its mouth was like the entrance to a secret passage, and frilled with pearl.

'If Blom puts this shell to his ear and listens carefully, he may hear the voice of the god of the mountain cult which I spoke of. It sounds like nothing much to me, but I am fairly deaf.'

'It is beautiful. What do you think the god of the mountain cult might say to a young prince whom he has never met?'

'I have no idea. Perhaps he will say that when Blom is married he must be sure to allow his wife to go into the mountains to sing and pull out her hair if she wants to.'

'Very instructive,' said the Akond. 'Well, I will give him the shell, and I shall revisit you on the occasion of the Second Gift, when we shall be able to observe the inclinations of his wife.'

The Akond took charge of the shell, imagining that he could hear from within it the thin wailing voice of the god of wild women. What would his son make of it, he wondered? These old gods, lost in the mountains of their exile, were always trying to catch the attention of their former devotees or to attract new ones. A cult of passion and rebellion was not something that he was eager to introduce into the palace. He smiled to himself as he wrapped the box containing the shell in several layers of rough baling, as if to muffle the trapped voice of the insidious god. It was a good thing, he thought, that he did not believe in the existence of gods.

And the Akond mounted his horse, and galloped back to the palace, where he discovered that Ininin had successfully accomplished all that had been asked of him.

At the ceremony of the First Gift, Blom was dressed for the first time in the silk coats of his princehood, jewelled at the neck. His robe was gathered up between his legs and tied with a scarlet cummerbund, and silken puttees were wound about his calves. He carried a little whip adorned with rubies.

The women of the palace gathered round him, as if to deliver him from their care. This was not quite the case, but in his eighth year Blom was to have a tutor, and would spend more time with his father, so they gave him tokens of their continuing affection, little trinkets that denoted a kind of farewell. Uz-Luba gave him a pillow; his grandmother uz-Mabmabla gave him a box of writing implements; his nurse gave him a coloured paper that folded into a bird; his mother gave him a box of sugared almonds; and he was given the shell from his grandfather.

A Tale

In the courtyard at noon all the palace servants gathered, and the Akond led the household on to the balconies to watch.

The Wazir clapped his hands, and a pair of grooms led in the First Gift on long silken bands attached to its bridle.

It was a spanking little filly of barely ten hands and of such unusual girth that she seemed almost as broad as she was long. She was as white as the sands of the desert, and her full mane and tail were plaited with green silk. She trotted round the courtyard at a great rate, snorting a little in her apprehension of the crowd, holding out her muzzle and chest like the figurehead of a ship, with green silk rippling behind her like flags. She was graceful in her fashion, but her legs were short and her belly full as a galleon.

Round she went sturdily at the end of the bands attached to her bridle, time after time, until the grooms led her to the centre of the courtyard where she waited patiently, breathing, chewing, tossing her head slightly until the young Akond was led down to her.

He was not expected to do anything more than touch her nose twice with his whip to acknowledge his ownership of her, although there were many present who well remembered how in-Blemim on the occasion of his First Gift had thrown himself at the flanks of his mare and had succeeded, after a few attempts, in mounting her and riding round the courtyard holding on to her neck, even though she had not been saddled.

Blom did nothing but stare, as though the whole of his imagined and difficult future life were somehow contained in this creature whose very breath was visibly exhaled from twin nostrils frighteningly damp and black, like snails. He had to be prompted to raise his whip and touch, with the ruby-cluster at its tip, the great slope of the filly's nose.

'Why, she is almost as fat as he is!'

The Akond's face darkened at this remark, not intended to be public, but none the less heard by most of those present. The observation was not made with malice, but it was true enough. And since it was made by a child, one of Anic's numerous offspring, in fact, there was nothing much to be done about it.

4

AT ABOUT this time there was terror in the villages of the forest of Wajlat, and it was both a terror of the thing known and a terror of things unknown, terror of the secret and terror of the dark. Even in the Elder's house, where a lamp burned through the night to remind the villagers of his importance.

'Come in, Sazzara. What are you doing?'

Bagril peered out into the dark from the crowd of flies that swarmed under the lamp on the verandah. He could not see his wife clearly, and did not know why she was outside at such an hour.

'Sazzara, Sazzara!'

A shape came towards him in the dark, a scarf over the mouth and hands clutching her elbows as if to avoid all contact with things of the night. His wife hurried up the verandah steps.

'What is it, Sazzara?' said Bagril. 'It is late. I must bolt the doors.'

'I thought something had got to the goats.'

'There is nothing wrong with the goats.'

'I thought there was something with the goats.'

'Something with the goats?' said Bagril. 'Do you mean someone with the goats? The goats are perfectly all right.'

And indeed, both of them could hear from the goats' open pen the rustling and the occasional peaceable tinkle of a goat-bell that indicated untroubled wakefulness and feeding.

'There has been someone with the goats before.'

'And have any goats been taken?' asked Bagril.

'Not to take goats.'

'Not to take goats,' repeated Bagril. 'To do what, then?'

His wife made no answer, since she was unwilling to explain her thoughts, and together they went into the house.

In a fire that suddenly shifts, sending up pennants of flame and betraying fresh wood with a crackle into the general glow, there are many shapes thrown up. They may be what you hope or fear, if you are staring for portents, or they may be the phantasms of memory, inevitable reminders of things already encountered.

The miner sees the rubies for which he daily toils, the woodcutter's child sees the face of her future husband, the baker's wife sees the baby who was abducted by wolves. While the fire glows, taking the chill off the evenings, warming the milk and honey placed by the hearth, it gives comfort by responding to fancy. A flame can waver slowly like the meditation it encourages, bringing a half-slumber; or it can shoot into dancing shapes that are like spirits let into the soul, bringing fresh notions to disturb the sleep later, when the fire is dying and the family has retired. In the small hours you may wake suddenly, and the fire of a fear is in your head, fixed with a wild certainty, though the hearth is now cold ash.

Sazzara would wake with the image of a child in her head, a child mysteriously flawed but still beautiful, like a gem that a bride attempts to pawn, defying the jeweller who is shaking his head critically, the magnifying eye-piece still screwed beneath his brow. But who, finding such a jewel to be flawed, would willingly lose it or cast it aside? Surely only someone who had appropriated it in the first place and feared to be found with it. And who might in a rare moment of tormented decisiveness have thought to dispose of it, and then immediately regretted the impulse? For if the jewel had already been rejected by its rightful owner as imperfect, why should it be twice abandoned? Isn't perfection for the most part an illusion? And isn't a major part of the right of ownership a full acquiescence in the nature of the object, whatever that might be?

And in any case, how may a child be abandoned, for whom the proprietorial love is unconditional? Wouldn't it be seen as so much of a mistake that it would count as an accident to be commiserated, rather than as an error to be explained?

Sazzara's terror was the recognition that in her case she had compounded the original error. Condemned by an absence, she forever conjured presences. How would a lost child survive? Kept in secret by others, out of pity? Confined, in disgust? Allowed to roam, in indifference? Lifting its thirsty mouth to the dugs of tolerant goats?

She had cared for it defiantly, against Bagril's wishes and later without his knowledge, until the Wazir himself had arrived at the Elder's house in anger. They had talked into the night, and Sazzara had not been permitted to sit with them, but had brought them salep, and had listened at the door.

It was only then that she understood how her brother, 'm Ezla, had come to lose his fingers. He had told her that he himself had accidentally cut them off while sawing green wood that was too slippery. But she knew that her brother was a scoundrel and a liar and she would not have believed him in any case, even if it were possible to cut off the fingers of the right hand with the right hand itself.

And she was afraid.

She was afraid of Bagril, whom she had disobeyed. She was afraid of 'm Ezla, though she knew he was ashamed of having spied on her to his own advantage. She was afraid for the old woman of the forest to whom she had taken the child. And she was afraid for the fingers of all her family.

She had gone to the old woman, who was already gripped by a terror of her own.

'You did not tell me that it was a child of demons!' the old woman accused Sazzara. 'It is an unclean thing!'

Sazzara could see that the old woman, against her explicit instructions, had loosened the swaddling about the child's body.

'I told you to keep it bound,' said Sazzara. 'It was not your business to open the child's body to the air.'

'You cannot keep a child in swaddling for ever,' said the old woman. 'It must move, and crawl, and then walk. For look: it is as though his feet are bursting out of his bonds in the very desire to walk. And yet –'

Here the old woman shuddered.

'And yet he has feet of his own, kicking there at the end of his legs! How many legs can he have?'

Sazzara was in tears.

'I told you that I could not keep the child,' she said to the old woman. 'Now it is the case that no one may keep it. It is too dangerous. I cannot tell you why, but you must believe me, and you must help me.'

'You cannot kill a child, however unclean,' said the old woman. 'The demons would take its soul. And then they would come for mine!'

'I will vouch for your soul,' said Sazzara. 'And you have the protection of my husband Bagril, who is the Elder.'

'I do not believe that your husband knows anything at all about it,' replied the old woman. 'Despite everything that you have told me, I think that it is your child, and that you have been consorting with demons.'

'We cannot kill the child,' said Sazzara. 'But we cannot keep it, and we must not speak of it.'

And together they left the child with provisions beside it deep in the adit of an abandoned mine.

'We have not killed it, and yet it cannot survive,' said Sazzara, in sorrow. And to herself she reflected that Bagril should have killed it in the first place, as he had been instructed, and that he should have told her nothing about it. And she gave the old woman enough money to keep her silence.

All this had happened years before, and yet Sazzara's terror brought visions of the return of the child. It was as if it were mysteriously immortal, perhaps the child of spirits after all, and not merely the strangest of the things from the palace that found their way into the possession of the Wazir's followers. She could not sleep for imagining the child returning to the lumber-room behind the dairy where she had once kept it, and the old verses of the poet came to her restless mind:

'The world that yields for the child that is made
Is the more for its making, the gods be praised.
The spirit asleep gives thanks for its waking
And the world will listen when voices are raised.

To the child that is hungry the world is a feast.
The hermit knows fasting, the gods be praised,
But the child will return to the milk of the beast

And the world will forgive as the gods stand
   dazed.

Chance is a cheater of joy, a hater
Of all that the heart (the gods be praised)
Wishes to welcome at the end of long waiting
And the gods will rescue, though the world is
   amazed.'

But Sazzara could say nothing to her husband, since
Bagril now truly imagined the child to be dead, and
he was restored to the Wazir's favour.

5

BUT JUST as it is written that our careful designs are as insignificant as a grain of sand in the stretches of the desert and as impermanent as web in the wind, the child did not die.

For the command that it should die was like a chain that is made up link by link in darkness out of scraps of metal that lie about, when the hand of the master craftsman is not in it, and the Akond had realised that the chain might not hold. For between the women of the bedchamber and uz-Mabmabla, the child's grandmother, there was the weakness of fear, and between uz-Mabmabla and the Akond there was the weakness of tenderness, and between the Akond and Ininin, his Wazir, there was the weakness of regret, and between him and Bagril there was the weakness of disrespect, and between Bagril and Sazzara there was the weakness of fondness, and between Sazzara and the old woman of the forest there was the weakness of guilt. And here and there were extraneous weaknesses such as the self-interest of 'm Ezla or the slim chances of natural survival. It is not easy to destroy a human being by mere neglect. A child found in the ruins of Biglat, eighteen days after the earthquake, lived from the seepage of a cracked vessel and the occasional encounter with beetles. In the world of the forest, darkness is not a product of disaster. Within it, the creatures learn to survive. The chances are not great, but what might be in the chain of cruel command a hairline crack, is in the natural struggle of the organism a chink through which the hope of survival may flood, like the sun piercing a dark and neglected forest glade.

It is not known how the child that the old woman had called unclean had survived. The villagers who had never seen it were inclined to call it a demon, for the unseen breeds the greater terror. The few who had seen it were divided in their opinion.

'It is a hairless wolf, living with wolves,' said one.

'But what wolf has ever been seen in a tree?' said another.

'It is an unusual kind of monkey,' said another.

'But what monkey has no tail?' said another.

'Or goes in and out of old mines?' said another.

'Or kills small creatures with a stick?' said another.

'It is a wild boy,' said another.

'But what boy clasps his young to his chest as he runs?' said another.

'That is not his young,' said another, shuddering. 'It is the remains of something that he has eaten. Which is still moving.'

There were those who pretended to have seen him, for the sake of the attention it would bring them. And since there was little point in such a claim without having something new to say, they invented incidents and descriptions.

'His matted hair reaches to his waist.'

'His yard is so long that it brushes the grass as he runs.'

'He devoured one of the Elder's goats and left nothing but the hooves.'

'His eyes are red and glowing like rubies.'

'He turned himself into wood-smoke and entered an empty olive jar.'

'He is an afreet who has taken imperfect human form.'

Any village child who was lazy or disobedient was told that if they did not mend their ways the afreet would come for them and eat them up, every scrap. Whereas if they were good, who knows but that they might be taken on a visit to the city to be bought sweetmeats and perhaps to see the young Akond riding in procession on his white horse.

The threats were intended as much to comfort the parents as to terrify the children, since the idea of a specific role for the afreet limited its otherwise almost illimitable powers. They had no intention of exposing their offspring to its rampant appetite, so they could safely turn it into a monitory ghoul largely of their own devising. Even so, there was always a moment of uncertainty before any of them opened a jar, and no one would now think to walk alone into the forest.

But there remained one man who would not only easily walk alone in the forest, but did little else, and that was an old prospector called 'l Saqi.

In his youth, 'l Saqi had worked on the dam at Sarapa and other engineering projects which the Akond of the time had commanded. He had learned to cut stone so accurately that one block could be laid upon another and would fit so tightly that there would be no need for mortar. The dam itself was built entirely without mortar, and its outer wall was always dry.

'l Saqi was amply rewarded by the Akond for his

skill, and was allowed to go south to develop the old ruby mines of Wajlat, which had failed for want of structure. He had personally selected his team of miners, tunnellers and engineers, and for many years the Akond's coffers were enriched with rubies. No longer did the entrances to the mines collapse, burying the miners who had burrowed too eagerly into the hillside. No longer did the tunnels peter out when the rock seemed impenetrable. The skill and patience of 'l Saqi conquered all such obstacles, and his team grew rich on those rubies which they saved for themselves.

But they became careless of their skills. Satisfied with the wealth they already possessed, they settled in the city, leaving many of their mines half-explored.

'With one of these gems that I already possess heaped about the house,' they would say, 'I can buy enough rice to last my family for a year. Why should I cramp my limbs and stifle my lungs by creeping into the mountainside with my pick and hammers?'

But 'l Saqi was proud and thorough. To find rubies in worthless rock was for him an end in itself, and every shaft and seam held out for him its absolute challenge. And 'l Saqi would make sure that it would be a challenge to the jeweller, too, for the miner could see in an instant the largest possible shape lurking within each uncut stone, and would prescribe its peculiar symmetry and faceting precisely. The jewellers feared and respected 'l Saqi, for if he required a polished gem the size of a hen's egg there was no use in keeping any small fragments back for themselves and giving him one the size of a pullet's egg. There was no use in claiming that any stone had broken, since 'l Saqi knew exactly where its flaws were, if any, and had made allowances for these.

He could not bear to think that any mine had been abandoned before it had yielded up all its glowing treasure, and he continued to work alone, no longer for profit but for perfection.

And it was this man, the engineer 'l Saqi, who found the abandoned boy. Only he, working patiently in the depths of the forest week after week, month after month, year after year, could become such a familiar presence that the two would eventually encounter each other without fear.

When they did, 'l Saqi was shrewd enough to pretend that he was not at all interested in the filthy tousled animal who crouched at a distance in the mouth of the cave, watching him closely. He simply went on chipping at the rock with regular strokes of his hammer singing quietly to himself:

> 'Old Owal, woodcutter,
> Loved mushrooms in butter . . .'

But of course he was interested. He had glimpsed him on many occasions, and knew of the tales in the village. He welcomed a closer look at this wild boy, who always ran clutching something to his chest, and who so far had eluded capture.

And so 'l Saqi continued to work, humming to himself, and now and then talking to the boy over his shoulder.

'I used to have friends once,' he said. 'But now I am quite alone.'

He could see the boy out of the corner of his eye, looking at him intently.

'Perhaps that's why you're not frightened of me,' said 'l Saqi. 'All alone, like you. Minding my own business in the forest.'

Very slowly, he turned his head to face the boy, and smiled.

The boy was now squatting, still staring up at him

with an interest that for the moment had conquered all other emotions, his arms at his chest, enclosing something that (did it?) stirred slightly.

Moisture dripped down from the roof of the working, leaving a gleaming surface on the rock, and setting a small fern to a regular nodding, like a mechanical time-piece. But time had nothing to do with this encounter. Time had absconded.

'l Saqi patiently applied his hammer.

'I don't suppose that you know how to smile, do you?' said 'l Saqi gently. 'Well, that's a great shame.'

The boy let out a sound, something between a groan and a hum, and ran one hand over his head, as though something disagreeable had landed there.

'Oh, I see,' said 'l Saqi reasonably. 'I didn't know that. Thank you.'

It pleased the old man to talk to the boy as though they were really communicating, for he had talked to no one else for months. And the boy squatted there as if he had known 'l Saqi all his life, and had nothing to fear from him.

'These stones I dig for,' said 'l Saqi. 'You see them?'

He held up an adamantine mass that glowed dully in the little light admitted by the cave.

A Tale

'They are created by fire from the rock,' he went on, 'and they are the mountain's eyes, looking out for the light, eager to draw it back into the earth. Like our eyes.'

And 'l Saqi pointed to his own eyes, bright beneath the brow of white hair.

The boy looked up at him, and raised a finger to his own face.

'That's right!' exclaimed 'l Saqi. 'Our eyes are the purest part of our body, fired by angels out of the human clay which surrounds them. Our eyes are the jewels of our soul!'

And he spoke the old mining verses of light and darkness, beating out the rhythms with his hammer:

'This is the light of life, incarnadine,
This is the light from the mouth of the mine.

In darkness the world collapses on itself,
Inward limbs and cowering spine.

But eyes are opened on darkness and they glow
Ineffable and crystalline.

Restless, they tear the darkness open
And its curtain becomes the colour of wine.

Darkness is the light we cannot see
Which rubies offer like a shrine.

We drink the darkness and make it shine.
This is the darkness that is divine.'

The boy crooned and moaned again, rocking on his haunches.

'You are no fool,' said 'l Saqi, 'I can see that. You are a lost boy, and the only men you have encountered have either chased you or run away from you. And if you accept some food from my knapsack, I do not know what will happen to us, for our path in life will surely be thereby joined irrevocably.

And 'l Saqi held out to him a small piece of bread from his knapsack, not knowing truly in his heart whether he wanted the boy to take it or not.

And the boy took it.

6

IT WAS the custom for the young Akond's horse to be brought to him every day by the grooms.

After bathing, Blom's pale body was oiled by his servant until it reflected the morning light dully, like a blanched almond. He was dressed in riding clothes, and taken down to the courtyard.

But Blom was frightened of his little horse, whose hooves disturbed the dust, and whose heavy body stirred and twitched beneath its bristly coat, as it patiently waited to be ridden. He did not see how he could lift himself on to it. He could not even raise his foot to the height of the stirrup, for he only had to imagine his garments straining uncomfortably against his groin in the act of doing so to believe it impossible.

The whole arrangement was ridiculous and impractical, like balancing a pear on a marrow.

What he much preferred to do was to retire with a bowl of fruit to his father's library, and to spend the morning reading old stories about birds who spoke to captive princesses, and merchants who made fatal bargains with djinns. He no longer wanted to play with his uncle Anic's sons or with the other children of the palace, since they now teased him in the most infuriating way imaginable, by showing him an exaggerated respect and keeping him at a distance. If he asked them to let him into a secret, to show him what they were doing, or to let him play, they bowed, feigning regret, and spoke in the formal tones of palace servants, then ran away giggling.

Blom was now enveloped in the haunted isolation of an heir. Even his nurse touched her forehead in his presence, and retreated to the quarters which were now forbidden to him.

His mother Juliba told him that he must bear himself with dignity, and diligently apply himself to the lessons of his tutor. This last he was happy to do, since he learned many things which intrigued him, but to bear himself with dignity? It seemed impossible in the body which had been provided for him.

His uncle Anic made a hoist for him, to enable him to mount his horse. Blom was to sit in a cloth sling and be winched to the required height within a wooden frame, part of which then swung out over the horse, lowering him on to it, like an armoured warrior before a battle. Blom allowed himself to be seated and lifted and lowered, but could not disentangle himself from the sling, which became caught in the horse's pommel.

Anic stood in the courtyard with his knuckles against his hips, roaring with laughter, as the horse turned round and round, and the rope of the hoist twisted itself against Blom's body.

In-Blemim saw this from the palace, and was angry with his brother.

'The boy must learn to make his own way in life,' he said, 'and does not need you to make a fool of him.'

'We are what we are by nature,' said Anic. 'Law or custom will not change it, though some personal effort might help.'

'You are proud of your own horsemanship,' replied his brother. 'You boast of it incessantly, as though it should give you rights which you imagine might be yours. But you will never be the Akond, just as I suspect that you will never challenge Dibl on the field of the goat. And you should not make fun of my son, for any reason whatsoever, for he will surely be the Akond and there is nothing that you can do about it.'

And Anic was silenced, and the hoist put away where it became a plaything for his children.

In-Blemim was puzzled by the character of his son, for though, as he said, he would surely be the Akond, had there ever been an Akond who could not ride a horse? When he reflected on this, he realised that his knowledge of Akonds was necessarily limited. He could remember his own grandfather, but had no reliable image of him on horseback. His father, uz-Blemim, was, as he came more and more to realise, now unusually sedentary. There was no reason, apart from his politically conventional exile in the administration of the spice plantations, why he should not take the time to journey to the palace to see his grandson. Any grandfather would do so, in genial defiance of old protocol. Was it that he was simply disinclined to make a journey of three or four days on horseback?

Perhaps it was only he himself, after all, thought in-Blemim, who positively enjoyed the poised energetic mobility of the gallop, the sensation between the thighs of the entire engine of the horse's body trembling in thunder beneath him? It was something he shared with his brother Anic that it might be unfair to expect from his son.

Blom was a dreamer, like his grandfather. And he took to spending hours of each day with his ear to the great shell that his grandfather had given to him. At first the carved box, with its padded silk lining that protected the shell, had been little opened. It had seemed, like many of his other presents, to be a purely decorative object, offered for its beauty rather than its function. But Blom had tired of toys, which he had come to associate with the quarrels of cousins. They were imperfect things, little mimicries of real life that were always breaking. The armless puppet, the missing wheel, the trailing string: Blom thought them sad relics of anger or neglect, and could feel no fondness for them.

But the shell was an unassailable and mysterious thing, which at once invited and excluded him. Held upright, its knotted spiral end was like the pointed helmet of an antique warrior from the north, whose depredations and ultimate defeat were depicted in some of the tapestries in the palace. Its lip was like a soft threshold, orange-pink and smooth like glistening flesh. When the shell was horizontal it seemed to invite him in, as though if he were small enough he could duck his head and crawl inside. And what would he find there? The sharp helmet seemed to locate a centre, like some defined military target, but the leisurely principle of the spiral suggested an infinite and repeated circling about a purely theoretical point, one that would never actually be reached. Once inside, he could continue to get smaller and smaller as he trod the delicious lining of the shell, and would never reach an end.

Or if there were somehow an ending to the shell, Blom thought, it would be such an extraordinary finality, such a revelation, that the shell would turn inside out, with him inside it, and then the new world would be all shell.

Nothing but shell, and he the master of it.

7

THERE WAS a merchant in the city of Taflat whose wife unaccountably died, leaving him with only one child. 'l Cara was inconsolable.

'I must be the wealthiest merchant in Taflat,' he sobbed. 'I have fifteen vessels upon the seas at any one time, sailing as far as Ormuz in the west and Cochin in the east. My house is the largest in Taflat, save for that of the mining engineer 'l Saqi, and he is never at home, for he has gone mad and lives in the forests of Wajlat. No one is respected more than I am, save for the Wazir of the palace, and that is after all for his office rather than his achievements. My father was a tiller of the soil, and I preside over a veritable empire of trade. But these vast possessions are of no value to me now that my wife has been taken from me.'

He stood weeping into the cloth that his wife had been embroidering when she was taken ill, and his tears stained the images of angels that held hands together all along the hem, save where the cloth was still a blank and as yet unsewn.

His friends took him by the arm and led him to a chair. They took the cloth from him and straightened its creases.

'You must eat,' they said, giving orders to his servants.

'How can I eat, when my wife can no longer eat?' he asked.

'You must continue to live for her sake,' they replied.

'How can anyone live,' protested the merchant, 'when the Envier of Delights may come at any time to take him away?'

The food was brought, a chicken stuffed with pomegranate seeds, and little cakes of almonds and syrup. 'l Cara pushed them away.

His friends brought in to him his little daughter, Ahraz.

'You must continue to live for your daughter's sake,' they said, 'for she is the very image of her mother, and her mother's spirit is in her.'

The merchant looked at Ahraz, whose beauty was already known in Taflat, though she was only five years old, and his heart melted once more. He was minded of the words of the poet:

A Tale

'The daughter's likeness from the mother
Lets them echo one another.

The mother in the daughter's face
Finds a kind of resting-place.

Winds of beauty making kin
Turn a cheek or touch a chin

Then to the horizons go
Where one can barely feel them blow

And where their dust deceives the eye
With tales that faces never die.'

And he took Ahraz in his arms and wept, and before nightfall he ate.

The cloth with the embroidered angels was sewn up at his instruction into a pillow, so that during his lonely nights he might rest his head at the blank place and fill it with his own dreams of the perfection of his dead wife. In visions he saw her taking her place in a dancing ring of these eternal spirits, and he spoke often of the visions to Ahraz.

'I did not deserve her,' he would say. 'She was too good for the earthly life, and the angels desired her company.'

Since Ahraz lived in a world already puzzling to her, where being good seemed to require the sacrifice of her own small interests to the whims of others, she could only conclude that these angels must be the most selfish and arbitrary creatures imaginable. Who could possibly want to join their company? Whenever she crept into her father's bedroom and glimpsed the sacred pillow, she regarded the gap in the bordering angels with satisfaction. Let them for ever seek to join hands, she thought. So long as their circle is broken and their dancing incomplete, then we mortals have a chance to lead our own lives, and to be naughty.

The extraordinary beauty of Ahraz, in the poise of her head, the depth of her eyes and the line of her jaw, gave her father much pride and concern.

'Of all my rich vessels,' he would say to his friends, 'she is the most precious. Trade enhances the value of cargo by removing it from one place to another, where it is more greatly desired. But her beauty has eternal value, and it is her own, and may never be negotiated.'

His friends objected.

'It is the greatest pleasure of fathers', they put to him, 'to see their daughters wed. Her beauty and your riches will make her a great prize, which surely must be negotiated.'

'Never,' said 'l Cara. 'I have lost my wife. Why should my only daughter be taken from me?'

'Surely,' said his friends, 'it will be the right of any suitable young man to woo your daughter in the fullness of time? Why, she is so beautiful that she may well be chosen as the bride of the Akond.'

'Piracy!' replied 'l Cara. And he would hear no more of such talk.

He became jealous of his daughter's freedom as she grew older, and did not allow her to leave the garden of his house. The servant who lodged at his front gate was instructed to refuse her if she asked to go out, even with her own attendants.

His friends remonstrated with him.

'If you cage her now,' they said, 'she will fly forever beyond your reach as soon as the cage is unlatched.'

But he would not listen to them.

Now it happened that the house next to 'l Cara's house, which had long been empty and shut up, save for the occasional attentions of servants, belonged to the prospector 'l Saqi. It was, as 'l Cara often complained, the only house in Taflat which was larger than his own, but so long as 'l Saqi was not in residence, the merchant was able for much of the time to forget the irritating fact of his neighbour's wealth.

One day there was a great bustle in 'l Saqi's house. The shutters were thrown open, and carpets beaten. A pack of mules arrived, laden with boxes which were taken into the house by servants, who staggered under the weight.

Ahraz, who had climbed her favourite tree in her father's garden, saw all this, hidden away among its leaves. It was to her the most interesting event that had occurred for a very long time, and she watched intently every morning to see what novelty might occur.

The great brass door of 'l Saqi's house was burnished brightly, and the gravel of his garden paths raked. New flowers freshly blooming were planted about the house, and the next day a thin column of blue smoke rose.

'They are baking at the house next door,' thought Ahraz. 'The owner must be returning.'

And sure enough, the very next day after that there appeared an old man with a long and untrimmed beard riding on a horse with heavy panniers. Sitting in front of him between his arms was a small boy wearing a burnous.

Ahraz was very excited, and ran to tell her father.

'Our neighbour has returned at last,' she said. 'And there is a little boy with him!'

Her father had seen all this for himself, and suspecting that 'l Saqi had returned from Wajlat with a Bedouin catamite, merely grunted. He had no intention of issuing any invitations.

Ahraz keenly observed the house next door over the following weeks. She noted that 'l Saqi had now shaped his beard. He appeared on the terrace of his house in a striking sky-blue robe very different from the working-clothes in which he had arrived. The boy, however, who ran about in the garden in a very peculiar way, still wore the clothes that he had arrived in, his head and shoulders completely shrouded with only the tender circle of his face showing. It made an effect all the more striking for being concealed, as the poet has written:

'The human face, a crown of power
Stands like a watchman on his tower.

It rides upon the labouring limbs,

Flawed Angel

Neighbour to artfulness and air.

The light adores it in its fashion,
Shaping with shadow all its features.

But in the dark it glows with passion,
The most expressive of all creatures.

Though we may loathe and clothe the clay
The face transcends it, and is fire.

Shroud it as we will, it shines
Out from our garments like a beacon

So the heart's needle turns towards it
And comes to do its bidding there.

It turns our deepest thoughts outside
And looks upon an everywhere.

Portal of our wish to act,
It opens at the break of day.

It finds itself in others' faces
And they in turn are what they see

And all the landscape of our lives
Stretches beneath their scrutiny.'

A Tale

The fountains now flourished freely in 'l Saqi's garden, and it seemed an inviting place. From the secrecy of her tree, Ahraz often saw 'l Saqi walking there with the boy, pointing to things with a stick as if he were showing him what they were. Sometimes she could hear 'l Saqi naming them, and encouraging a response from the boy.

And the boy would nod violently, clutching himself.

'l Saqi would repeat the word.

'Vase,' he said. 'Vase.' And he tapped a large earthenware jar with his stick.

The boy looked up in agony to the heavens, grinning wildly.

'Vase. Vase,' repeated 'l Saqi.

The boy moaned, apparently with pleasure.

'He does not know the words,' thought Ahraz. 'He must be a foreigner from the West, from Persia, perhaps. But he cannot say any words, not even the words in his own language. How can he not have any words? He is older than I am.'

The boy continued to roll his head.

'Perhaps he is not a boy at all,' thought Ahraz. 'Perhaps he is a wood-demon brought back from the forests of Wajlat. But he has a beautiful face.'

She was haunted by the boy's staring eyes gleaming from the moon-like disc of face surrounded by the burnous, and fascinated by the infinite patience of the old man. At first she longed to make herself known to them, and to join in their word games, but she was afraid of what her father might say.

There was a moment when the boy's restless eyes seemed to pause when they passed her tree, just visible over the wall of her father's garden. She did not know whether to make a movement or not. She did not know if she had been seen.

She did not after all know if she wanted to be seen.

8

ONE DAY, the manager who had been the under-manager of the spice plantations came running to the old Akond's palace. He was admitted, and hastily bowing his forehead to his master's slippers he exclaimed: 'Exaltedness, there is a troop of armed men riding below in the valley!'

Uz-Blemim raised both his eyebrows at once in an exaggerated imitation of surprise. He looked at the manager in expectation. He was entirely used to receiving all information in the context of practical proposal. The manager might say: 'Exaltedness, the pruning in the upper fields west of the great gorge has revealed some rot. I suggest some partial replanting.' And all the old Akond had to do was to nod, and say: 'I approve.'

But on this occasion all that the manager did was to look back at uz-Blemim in equal expectation. So they stared at each other.

Ever since his son's last visit, the old Akond had taken comfort from the idea that it was futile to complain of having used up a third of his remaining portion of life when two-thirds remained. For a few years he even began to think that he might be in a position to have things to look forward to, if only he could learn to stop regretting the past, and he began to amass for himself in his private coffers the gold which his son sent him as payment for the consignments of spice. He might build a new palace in Samira, he thought, or a little further away at Abba or Amora, with vast apartments and new entertainments. A palace of pleasure for himself would be a strange but intriguing plan. Might it help him to remember what pleasure actually was? The lines of the poet came to him in the evening hours:

'What does the body do
Being flesh all through?
The body makes its peace.
The body makes its plea.
It gladly signs the lease
Of its short tenancy.

Welcomes the flickering light,
The harem scents at night,
The honey and the milk,

A Tale

The secret touch of walls
That yield, and from its silk
The voice that quietly calls.

Inviting light that shone
From palace windows on
The world that lay outside,
Calling the dark indoors,
Each pleasure like a bride
With her ambassadors.

O sensual visitors,
The heart throws wide her doors.
The spirit like a guest
Approaches to adore you.
By you the heart is blest.
The heart is sighing for you.'

It was in the midst of trying to remember, and of sketching some designs of hunting lodges, mazes, and pavilions of love, that he suddenly realised one day that his son's advice could no longer be followed. It was in the middle of the fourth year after the ceremony of the First Gift, when the dark thought crossed uz-Blemim's mind like the shadow of a vulture over a watering-hole: there was now no more of his life left than had already passed since the birth of his grandson had turned him upside-down like an hour-glass and set the grains in motion. They shifted and trickled through the narrow neck of experience, always passing too quickly to be observed, however hard he tried. Quickly and inexorably!

Now the occasion of the Second Gift would arrive in the same amount of time that had already passed since the occasion of the First Gift, which to uz-Blemim seemed no time at all. And it was like the intense sadness of the passing of a long afternoon, where the morning has been completely wasted. Thus it was that the old Akond was often to be seen sitting and staring into the dark corners of the rooms where he chose to be, or where he found himself, for he was hardly aware of making any significant choices in respect of his daily life. His servants had their orders, so that the small events of his existence never failed to occur. The largest event, which could occur only once, was something which he would have to do for himself, and he trembled at it.

'Excellency,' said the manager, 'what should be done?'

Together they walked out on to the terrace and looked out to the valley, but nothing could be seen.

They walked further, down through the palace gardens and past the manager's house. They walked to an outcrop of rock and looked further down the valley, where a small trail of dust showed them where the horsemen were passing.

It was hard to tell how many men there were down there.

'How do you know that they are armed?' asked uz-Blemim.

'When I first saw them I could see muskets,' said the manager.

'Ah, muskets,' said uz-Blemim. 'Well, well. Can we get a horseman ahead of them, do you think? By sending him first along the upper path?'

'He would have to ride as far as Samsela,' said the manager. 'And he would have to leave within ten minutes at least.'

'You will have to go yourself,' said uz-Blemim. 'And warn my son, the Akond.'

'I am no great horseman,' said the manager, in fright. 'Even if I make good time to Samsela, it is likely that they will see me, and give chase.'

'Go!' said the old Akond. 'And take the best horse.'

'The horse will be exhausted long before I can reach the Akond's palace,' said the manager.

'Take this purse,' said the old Akond, 'and change horses when you have to. Go, go! You are not my manager for nothing.'

The horse was saddled, and the manager, tying up his hair in a white cloth, left after twelve minutes. At Samsela he descended to join the road in the valley, stumbling frequently in the rocky path, turning the horse from left to right, losing his grip on the bridle, dislodging stones.

When he came to the valley road he galloped in a southward direction, but almost immediately saw the armed troop already a way ahead of him. There was no possibility of warning the Akond without over-taking them, whereupon they could easily capture him or perhaps kill him immediately. But if he simply turned back he would have failed the old Akond, and the soldiers would continue down the valley. Who knows what havoc they might cause on their way? They might be intending an assault upon the palace.

In the time it took to reflect upon all this, and before he could make up his mind as to what he should do, the manager found he was close enough to be heard and seen, and one of the riders had turned to meet up with him.

From the shoulders down it was a French

infantryman in tattered blue coat with torn red cuffs and epaulettes, a dead rabbit hanging from his bandoleer. But from the neck upwards he had an Ottoman appearance, with dark eyebrows, a sun-burned face and a bulging turban. He had a musket slung across his back which the manager was glad to see he made no attempt to reach.

'My good friend,' said the infantryman, 'my name is Captain Orqueban. Perhaps you can tell me where we are. Is this the valley of the Indus?'

The manager understood no French, but was relieved at the soldier's friendly smile. After some misunderstandings they found that they could converse a little in Turkish, and Captain Orqueban learned that he and his companions were by no means in the valley of the Indus, that it was far away, and that this was not the way to reach it.

What to do? It would seem that out of both hospitality and caution the manager should not let this party proceed alone. But should he take them back to the old Akond at Samira, or should he accompany them to the palace of the Akond himself, where the Akond's guard could keep an eye on them if they intended mischief? From Taflat, indeed, they might procure a sail for Karachi, if they had the means. And there were too few of them to make trouble.

'The old Akond expected me to ride to his son, and will be angry if I return,' thought the manager. 'But if I go with them, will they kidnap me?'

His mind was made up by an offer of gold from the leader of the troop, Colonel Marzipol, who had ridden back to join his captain. The manager was to become their guide.

And after a few days he was able to bring them before the Akond.

9

THERE were times when 'l Saqi almost despaired of civilising his wild boy, whom he had named 'l Isilik, 'the unknown one'. His servants were frightened of him, and would not wash him or do anything for him. His handsome face and darting manner sometimes distracted from the weight of his deformity, which, though his dress always kept it well hidden, troubled those who came into his company. For 'l Saqi, who was now accustomed to it, it was a matter of infinite pity. It was for this, he knew, that the child had been abandoned, as it had been his own destiny to find him in all his starving filth, hugging his shame before him, ready despite fear to accept food. It was for 'l Isilik's sake, he came to believe, that he had remained for so long in the old mines of Wajlat, looking for something besides rubies. And something told him that the joy he took in 'l Isilik's restoration to the human world, the eagerness in learning and the excitement of discovery, the shining in his eyes and the readiness of his tongue, could only be bought at a price, just as life itself can only be obtained in the shadow of death. If 'l Saqi had unaccountably gained in old age the son he had never any right to expect, something told him that his gratitude was always destined to be qualified by the pain of 'l Isilik's hideous imperfection. He did not deserve to have the one without the other.

Years passed, and 'l Isilik came to be able to converse, and to count, and to sit before meat, and to perform all those tasks that keep a being clean and in confidence of a comfortable existence. From being able to respond to simple questions and point to named objects, he progressed to the recognition of abstract ideas and the expression of his own needs and feelings. He was none the less very quiet, and his longest utterances were the rhymes which little children love, and which 'l Saqi felt that he invested with a significance of his own. He took particular delight in:

'The name with no face
Took up no space,
But the face with no name
Was himself just the same.'

and in:

> 'One, two, three, four, five:
> Where will the swimmer dive?
> Six, seven, eight, nine, ten:
> Into the fire and back again.
> Will he tell you where he's been?
> Will he tell you what he's seen?
> Only if you kiss him nicely.
> You'll not need to ask him twice.'

When reciting this one, 'l Isilik would shut his eyes, expecting to be kissed. And he liked 'l Saqi to recite 'Old Owal', joining in himself for the last line, and repeating it emphatically:

> 'Old Owal, woodcutter,
> Loved mushrooms in butter.
> "Ouch!" said the maggots
> As he fired the faggots,
> "Old Owal is callous
> To gobble our palace."
> Old Owal said: "Cease
> Your mutterings, please.
> Go back to the wood

Where your palaces stood.
They stand there still."'

'They stand there still' was repeated slowly, with a sense of mystery.

But 'l Isilik could not be brought into society without scandal, and 'l Saqi began to be troubled by thoughts of what might happen to him after his death. He had the boy named as his heir, but knew very well that it would be a long time before 'l Isilik could acquire the knowledge and the confidence to manage the complicated running of his household, even to maintain the loyalty of his servants, who were in awe of him. 'l Saqi frequently kept to his bed with a weakness of disposition and feared the time when he could no longer oversee his servants or look after the well-being of 'l Isilik.

Now 'l Isilik had indeed seen the beautiful Ahraz in her tree that day, and ever afterwards looked for her in her garden. He found a place in the old wall between the gardens of the two houses where the mortar had already fallen away, and where by scraping it further and removing a stone he could make a chink large enough to look through.

The garden of 'l Cara had become a wild place. In

his continued mourning he neglected to give orders to his servants. The house was unclean, the terraces were unswept, the trees unpruned, the paths unwatered. Lizards clasped the walls like misers clasping their coffers of gold.

And Ahraz, though similarly confined, was not loved with a father's generous love, for as she grew older she came more and more to resemble her dead mother, though outshining her in beauty, and sometimes 'l Cara could hardly for this reason bear her to be in his presence.

'l Isilik often went to his chink in the wall, hoping to catch sight of Ahraz. And sometimes he did see her, at a distance, as though framed in some melancholy miniature, and he would speak in a low voice through the chink, words that he would never have addressed to her directly.

'Fair vision, lovely child, you are like a reflection of me in your empty garden. It is for you that the roses clamber in such profusion, for you that the jacaranda weeps. Leaves fall in the pool, and the fish are blinded from the neglect of you. You are like a ruby glowing from the walls of a forgotten mine, where there is no one to see you, let alone to dislodge and claim you. You may not leave the garden, for 'l

Cara is jealous of your beauty; I may not leave the garden, because I know I am strange. I have a secret at my heart which makes me like no one else in the whole world. And here is our destiny: to be placed next to each other like rare animals in their enclosures.'

He could not find words for all these ideas, but the feelings which brought them into his head were real enough. He did not know that Ahraz had feelings of her own, looking down on him at different times from different branches of her secret tree, which was now so tangled and uncared-for that she was quite invisible within it. These were the words in her head.

'Strange vision, lonely child, you are like a reflection of me in your empty garden. It is for you that the paths twist and turn and all lead into the centre, for you that the fountain climbs like a wet fist grasping for the sky. Your face is mirrored in the pool, and the sun is blinded by its reflection. You are like a dancing angel reaching out for company, but there is no one to see you, let alone to take your hand. You may not leave the garden, for 'l Saqi is jealous of your power; I may not leave the garden, because I am guilty of the death of my mother. I have a spell upon my face which makes me like no one else in the whole world. And here is our destiny: to be placed next to each other like objects in a museum.'

And so, each from his secret place, through a chink in a wall, from a leafy tree, the pair watched each other without communicating, sharing a mysterious sense of destiny.

At length, just as vagrant souls find only imperfect human shape and just as eternity is measured out in days each as hopeful and unsatisfactory as the last, so the destiny of Ahraz and 'l Isilik was for a moment resolved by events which drew them apart from each other.

As predicted by 'l Cara's friends, and no doubt effectively engineered by them, the Wazir's agents came to his house asking to see Ahraz. 'l Cara was angry, and at first refused, but was politely told that refusal in this case was impossible. Their report of Ahraz's beauty so impressed Ininin that he himself went to the merchant's house at Taflat to see her.

Over thimbles of thick coffee flavoured with cardamoms they stared at each other with icy politeness.

'You understand,' said Ininin to 'l Cara, with just the slightest curl of a smile beneath his great nose, 'that if she is chosen as the consort of the Second Gift, there is nothing that you can do about it. A father should be proud at the mere possibility.'

'l Cara shuddered.

'Proud that she might become the plaything of the young Akond? She has scarcely put away her own playthings, and she is not yet a woman.'

'She is already rigged for the voyage of womanhood, and waiting for a fair wind,' replied Ininin. 'And she may not refuse such a captain.'

'l Cara knew that he could not obstruct the Wazir's intentions, for that would displease the Akond. He also knew that a father was compelled not only to sacrifice his daughter to the wishes of the Akond, but to pay in addition an immense dowry into the palace coffers, proportionate to his wealth. When the Wazir's agents came again to inspect his books and to assess the profits of his trade, 'l Cara knew that further opposition was futile. The sum had to be paid, even though as a consequence he was himself unable to pay the captains of his vessels when they returned to the harbour at Taflat from Africa, laden with ivory, gold dust, gums and slaves. They came to the gates of his house, shouting and protesting, but were turned away by the porter.

'It is no use your coming here,' said the porter.

'My master will see no one since his daughter was taken away by the Wazir. He has retired to his bed in utter sorrow.'

'What are we to do?' said the captains. 'After long voyaging we need to return to our families. We have impounded the cargoes, but what can we do with them?'

'Perhaps you can set up as merchants for yourselves,' replied the porter, 'for I believe that is how it is usually done. And I would be obliged if you would bring me a bale of something that I can sell, for I, and indeed all the servants, have not been paid for months.'

But the captains were angry, and threw stones into the merchant's garden before they eventually left.

'l Saqi heard all this at a distance from his day-bed in the adjoining house, to which he had retired with a weakness of his lower back.

'These are changing times,' he thought. 'Miners who laboured for me, unskilled men of no training or culture, are now men of substance as a result of their long filching in Wajlat. My servants no longer obey me, and are simply waiting for me to die, so that they can seize my house from 'l Isilik. And now the gates of my neighbour, 'l Cara, an illustrious man and the wealthiest merchant in Taflat, are besieged by his creditors, rough sailors for the most part, little more than opportunists and adventurers.'

He sent for his chief servant, 'm Fega.

'I am not long for this world,' said 'l Saqi. 'And when I am gone, I want you to serve my ward, 'l Isilik, as faithfully as you have served me. He is my heir in law, and will inherit my property.'

And 'm Fega bowed deeply as if in full acknowledgement of these instructions, but said nothing. In his heart he knew that he could not serve 'l Isilik, whom most of the women servants thought was a wood-demon brought from the caves of Wajlat. In fact, if their master died, they all believed that 'l Isilik would tear off his handsome mask and be revealed in his full dripping horror.

And 'l Saqi, knowing this, fell back on his bed in sadness, and dismissed his servant.

The two men, merchant and engineer, neighbours and no friends, were now in a similar situation, more and more confined to their beds, distracted by age, fearful for their riches, and grieving for their heirs, whose future now seemed uncertain of happiness and not to be shared by the old men who loved them most.

10

'SO,' SAID said Colonel Marzipol, after a dinner entirely and ingeniously composed of goat. 'You will welcome us, poor adventurers as we are?'

The Akond beamed and nodded. Marzipol's men had been accommodated within the barracks of the Akond's personal Guard, and the Colonel, with his two officers, Captain Orqueban and Captain Debussy, were his guests at the palace.

An interpreter, brought in by the Wazir from Taflat, went to work. He was a schoolteacher, son of a trading family from Belle Isle, known for his ability to speak many languages. He followed the conversation as closely as he could, and provided the sense of it to each party, but he had that evening eaten as much as he had eaten in the previous four days, with wine to match, and did not always understand precisely.

'Ah, yes,' said the Akond, after a moment. 'To seek one's fortune is a noble endeavour, and I can understand the betrayal of allegiance given the prospect of gold.'

There was a similar pause while the schoolteacher translated as best he could, and so it continued, save for a few moments of longer pause, when the schoolteacher, chewing laboriously, was obliged to relieve himself of a segment of glutinous tail bone.

'It is we who were, in a sense, betrayed,' said Colonel Marzipol, 'so that it seemed perfectly legitimate to detach ourselves. Every man for himself is a fine motto in an emergency.'

'We should like to hear your history,' said the Akond. 'Your case is in a sense desperate. You lead your ragged troop over one deep valley after the other, thinking only of the next ridge, and you find us by chance, imagining that you have reached the great Indus. We are flattered, of course, but how did you know that we would not simply cut you to pieces?'

'We threaten no one,' said Colonel Marzipol. 'Our muskets are shouldered and cold.'

'And our swords have gems and edges,' replied the Akond. 'But we believe in reason. We are free with our favours, at peace with ourselves and our friends. Come. Your story.'

The Akond motioned to a footman to replenish the Colonel's beaker, but it was politely refused. Marzipol was a slight man with bristling fair moustaches brushed upwards into brief triangular shapes like the sails of a yacht. He was wound like the spring of a watch, and moved with a contained energy that manifested itself in precise and regular movements. His hand covered his beaker, then he smiled up at the footman, then he patted his mouth fastidiously, then he coughed, then he began.

'You will understand', he said, 'that our great General Bonaparte has a vision of a new world sustained by French culture and learning. We entered Egypt as both the cradle of civilisation needing the scholarly attention of our savants, and as a vital military possession. With Egypt under our control, the Ottoman Empire would totter and the English in India be terror-struck. Nor could the English control the Mediterranean for long.

'But we were betrayed. General Kléber was assassinated and the command passed to General Menou, a ridiculous incompetent without military vision. He seemed more interested in settling down to domestic life in Alexandria than in repelling the English: he married a local bathkeeper's daughter and himself adopted the religion of Mahomet. When the English did come, against all odds, he mismanaged the resistance completely. But our greatest betrayal came from our navy. Of course, Bonaparte sent reinforcements, but Admiral Ganteaume was too frightened to land them. Twice the fleet approached, twice it went away again.

'We had little influence over the Turks, who were ready to welcome the English, and less over the Mamelukes who are always a law unto themselves. After a ridiculous stand-off at Rhamanieh, my company retreated to Cairo, whereupon the generals surrendered completely. But my platoon had not retreated to Cairo. We crossed the Nile and headed east.

'It is easier than you think in time of war to become invisible, if you want to. If you are stopped, you can frequently bluff even without written orders, and it is perfectly possible simply to pretend that you are travelling in the opposite direction. In truth, most of our countrymen were eager to go home, and accepted the terms of the capitulation readily. No one, English, French or Turk, could believe that a colonel with a detachment of fourteen men was simply heading off into the desert. Our conduct gave special meaning to the notion of desertion.'

(Mild choking from the interpreter, who was

having some trouble in keeping up in any case, and was confounded by the pun.)

'It is clear that Bonaparte's intention had been, like Alexander the Great, to follow the courses of the Euphrates and the Tigris from Aleppo to the Persian Gulf, before he was unfortunately stopped at Acre. From the Gulf he would have proceeded to the Indus. I cannot say that this is exactly what we have done, since, as you have discovered for yourself, it is very easy to get lost.

'But just as it is easy to get lost, it is perfectly easy to proceed. A great army will raise the opposition of any alert ruler, who will have his informants vigilant at every outpost. But a platoon of fourteen men? It will excite local curiosity only. As for fear of being cut to pieces, we have the surgeon of our demi-brigade with us, Captain Debussy here, and two of his orderlies with their field-cases of instruments intact. Wherever we have been, far from being the cause of violence, we have brought medical relief in a spirit of fraternity, consonant with the ideals of our great Revolution.

'The brilliant Alexander failed, and General Bonaparte failed, even though he has brought the Emperor of Austria to his knees, and has the English scuttling about the Mediterranean not knowing at all what they are doing. He will draw back the better to spring forward later, but meanwhile here we are as harbingers of liberty and reason, grateful for your hospitality.'

Colonel Marzipol bowed at the end of all this, and indicated with his hand the surgeon, Captain Debussy, to whom he had made reference. Captain Debussy, a man of pasty and portly appearance, distinguished by enormous black drooping moustaches, also bowed, and raised his beaker in a friendly way to the Akond and to the company in general.

Anic, who had been sitting quietly for the whole evening, now laughed.

'This is an entirely amazing story,' he said. 'Are we to believe that you have travelled, what, upwards of two thousand miles, through the great empires of the Sultan Selim and Zaman Shah and Fath 'Ali Shah and through countless smaller kingdoms, without encountering the least opposition?'

'That is so,' replied Colonel Marzipol. 'We have done good service, and our fame has preceded us.'

'Not here, I think,' said Anic.

'Well, sir, said Colonel Marzipol, 'it may be that

here you live in greater isolation from your neighbours, finding news of any kind of little interest. We present no threat, and are entirely self-sufficient as soldiers trained to live off the land can always be. For us in this great adventure, life is lived in a continual state of emergency. Unlike most visitors from the West, we offer no outrage to your religion, having none ourselves, since the Directoire has done away with it.'

There was a slight gasp at this statement, and Ininin, the Wazir, said stiffly: 'Religions may be less outraged by toleration than by abolition.'

'Quite so,' said Colonel Marzipol, unperturbed. 'I did not mean to suggest that religion could not be tolerated. It would, I think, be intolerable if it were not tolerated.'

Another pun! The schoolmaster almost swallowed a date stone.

'It is, after all,' continued Colonel Marzipol, 'reason and science which represent the direction of the greatest progress in society. I have been welcomed in the countries through which we have travelled, for my skill in the construction of small bridges. And Debussy here, of course, is a genius of medicine, which is, as I am sure we would all agree, the greatest and most humane of all the sciences. The scalpel is mightier than the sword.'

'But what is it that you want from us?' asked Anic, suspiciously.

'I have to confess', said Colonel Marzipol, 'that since it is perfectly clear that we find ourselves here by accident, we can hardly claim to want anything at all.'

'You really expect us to believe that?' asked Anic.

But before Colonel could reply, the Akond, who had been silent all this while, leaned forward earnestly, and asked: 'Can you cure the toothache?'

11

ENTERTAINMENTS were to be provided for the guests, beyond custom, and at expense. Dancing girls were recruited and drilled by uz-Mabmabla in the age-old ceremonies of whirling and erotic invitation. The palace cook sent to the dam at Sarapa for fresh-water fish, which were brought back in ice-wagons. A giant octopus, which had been caught by a clipper off Muscat and had cost the lives of six sailors in bringing it back to Taflat, was commanded by the steward, and brought to the palace packed in salt. The court magician was ordered to rehearse a new demonstration of his skills, and the impresario 'm Baz invited to bring his theatre to the palace to perform one of the Akond's favourite classical plays.

Ininin suggested to the Akond that he should not go too far in such provisions for his guests.

'Such things may be suitable for impressing an emissary from Tipoo Sultan, or some obliged Caliph,' he said. 'But these are, after all, vagabond soldiers, who would be shot by their general were he ever to come across them.'

But in-Blemim silenced his Wazir.

'Peace, Ininin,' he said. 'I believe that General Bonaparte would regard our guests as enterprising emissaries rather than adventurers, and it would be as well to treat them as such. Besides, you know very well that Captain Debussy has cured me of a life-long toothache that the palace barber was too terrified to do anything about. I am obliged to him, and to laudanum, for the truce in my poor jaw, and he alone is worth the celebration of any treaty.'

But then the Wazir spoke again.

'Are you not in danger, Exaltedness,' he said, 'of anticipating the great celebration of the Second Gift? The time is not far off, and you would not, for the young Akond's sake, wish to arrange for him a lesser display of delights?'

But in-Blemim again silenced his Wazir.

'No, Ininin,' he said. 'These occasions for festivity are few enough. We may regard our preparations now as a mere rehearsal for those to come when Blom is of an age to receive the Second Gift. You have secured the girl already, and she is safely hidden in the women's quarters? She will therefore learn much at an early stage from uz-Mabmabla, and be thoroughly prepared. Besides, as you know, I am concerned that Blom shows little interest in the pleasures and privileges of his situation. Our present entertainment may go some way, I hope, to exciting him a little.'

But Blom was not only never excited, he did not seem to be interested in the possibility of excitement. He did not seek it. He did not notice its absence from his life.

His preferred occupation was reading, but all the fantastical stories that he read simply made him sad.

'What on earth is the use,' he would say, 'of struggling against all odds to achieve happiness, to overcome the cunning of merchants, the jealousy of stepmothers, the faithlessness of wives, the greed of demons and the riddles of djinns, only to find that in the end you are powerless to put off the arrival of the great Spoiler of Content?'

'Blom,' said in-Blemim, with a sigh, 'you are the true heir of your grandfather.'

And the Akond brought jugglers and dwarfs before his son, to tumble and hit each other with bladders on sticks, and to make him smile. But Blom turned away and would not smile.

He wondered if there were a solution to the mystery of life, that achieved such momentary elaboration, like the startling shimmer of the humming-bird's wings, only to disappear a moment later, and be gone for ever. Did the monuments of the dead contain any clue to that mystery? He often looked at his shell and wondered about the creature to whom it had belonged. It must have been quite unlike the inhabitants of shells that he had eaten, squat headless things, all slime and stomach, barely deserving to exist at all, living in simple crusted hovels that could be opened like books, where everything was plain to see, before being tossed on the kitchen midden. The inhabitant of his grand-father's shell must, compared with these, have been an Akond of his kind, for his surviving monument was a pink palace. And when he held it to his ear he heard a distant whispering voice, cold as the sea or the distant peak of a mountain, telling him things that sometimes he felt he could almost understand. Where did the voice come from? Was it perhaps the voice of the creature who had lived inside, bodiless now, translated into pure sound? Or was it his grandfather's voice, speaking urgent truths to him, but quietly and with the feeble insistence of age and

approaching death? He had never met his grandfather, but knew that he lived, as he had to, far in the
north, where rivers gathered in the coldness of rock
and brought life in a fragile cycle to the valley below.
The shell was perhaps the spirit of that mountain,
with its strange story of origins, like the old verses:

'The shell widens like a blind eye
(Weave the wind, weave the wind).
It opens on its milky sky
(Weave the wind with water of the waves).

The shell shuts on its gristle
(Dye the clouds, dye the clouds).
It closes, clean as a whistle
(Dye the clouds with its dead colour).'

The Akond took the French soldiers hunting, but
Blom was not of the party. He could now, of course,
mount his little horse with no need of the sling, nor
any other assistance. But he could not often be
induced to do so, and on the rare occasions when he
did, sat impassively upon it in much the same way as
he used to sit in his cousins' toy wagon and let himself
be pulled. The little horse might occasionally make a
half-turn, or snort, or look longingly towards the

horizon, but she grew to expect nothing from her rider, and was contented to bear him on her back while she nosed about for some weed which could be worth eating. Blom might just as well have been seated on a divan, except for the absence of a plate of quince jellies, or a cushion or two for his head.

Colonel Marzipol looked admiringly at the Akond's horse as they galloped together in the wake of some decorative birds that whirred up into the sky like wind-up toys.

They met in a little thicket, and waited while the Akond's servants ran about the meadows collecting the coloured corpses. Steam rose from the animals' flanks.

'Pure *Arabia felix*, I imagine,' said the Colonel. 'Such a breed was very difficult to be procured in Egypt, and the price would have been above 600 *Louis d'or*.' He pointed to the horse.

'Oh, you're talking about my horse, are you?' said the Akond. 'He's a real Yemen stallion. Genealogy certified by the sherif of Mecca.'

The Akond leaned forward to pat the horse's neck. The Colonel nodded and smiled, but hadn't understood more than two words. He was determined to acquire the language, and resolved to take lessons from the schoolteacher. There was much of interest in this little kingdom, and its ruler seemed entirely well-disposed towards him. Why shouldn't he for the time being settle here and establish French interests and influence where they might ultimately have some effect? Such as access to magnificent horses?

It took two hours to gallop round the private park of the palace, which the Akond's party performed with much gaiety, with flags fluttering and snare-drums beating, and with loud whoops from Anic. Meanwhile, the birds had been conveyed to the palace and prepared for the evening's feast. Stuffed with each other, and with pine-nuts, honey, vinegar and spices, they were spit-roasted in the open air, where music was played, and fireworks splashed streaming light upon the inky sky.

12

IN THE harbour at Taflat lived many men who worked on the boats: ropemakers, chandlers, riggers, caulkers, fitters, carpenters, dockers, victuallers, sailors. Their work was hard and repetitive, their hours long, their pleasures crude and simple. At night they drank in the brightly lit houses of pleasure in the alleys behind the waterfront, losing and sometimes gaining small silver at the throw of the dice. The servants of wealthy households frequented such places, for many goods could be negotiated there at prices far below those asked at the market, and the difference pocketed. For every cargo was taxed by the Akond, whose officer of customs kept account of everything that entered (or left) Taflat, and every merchant did all in his power therefore to minimise the official size of his cargo. If some of this illicit and unofficial cargo went missing, there was not much that the merchant could do about it, for no one could be accountable for what had never been accounted for.

A Tale

The major-domo of the household of the engineer 'l Saqi was a man who had been frequently seen at the waterfront. 'm Fega was used to supplementing his wages in this way, particularly as for years his master had not been at home and had been unable, therefore, to scrutinise 'm Fega's accounts personally. Since his return, however, 'l Saqi had kept a close watch on his domestic affairs, and 'm Fega was frustrated.

The dealers in misappropriated cargoes would sidle up to him on the bench, offering him wine or salep.

'It's no use,' 'm Fega would say. 'I can no longer deal with you. My master is a man of diligence and probity. He examines all my accounts now that he has returned to Taflat. Even in his illness he demands to see all receipts.'

'We can provide you with receipts,' they said.

'No,' was 'm Fega's reply. 'It's pointless. They would be the wrong receipts. He would know immediately. He is a man who seems to enjoy paying his taxes. I would be dismissed.'

'That is unfortunate for you, 'm Fega,' they said, and would treat him to a glass of salep in any case.

One day, such a dealer approached the major-domo, who sat in some relative splendour in the livery of his employment, drinking coffee and eating small cakes. The dealer was an outright smuggler, eager to get the goods off his hands.

'Three bales of Madras cotton, sir,' said the smuggler. 'Only four gold pieces a bale.'

'What do I want with Madras cotton?' replied 'm Fega. 'Am I a tailor?'

'Dried Chinese plums?' said the smuggler. 'Salted fish?'

'Look,' said 'm Fega. 'I'm tired of having to explain. My master is a man of rectitude. I can make no profit from illicit goods. Come to me in a month's time and things might be different. He is virtually on his death-bed and has left his estate to a wild boy, a freak of nature that he found in the forests of Wajlat. The boy can barely talk, let alone read. I shall have no problems once my master has left this world.'

In his irritation and sense of frustration with his position, 'm Fega had raised his voice, and was overheard by a group of shipbuilders and carpenters nearby. They mocked him.

'No wonder you're sitting there with such a gloomy face!'

'A freak of nature for a master? Whoever heard of such a thing?'

'It sounds as though your problems will only be beginning.'

'Who'd be a servant anyway? Better to sell your labour to the highest bidder and keep your freedom.'

'What sort of freak? Wajlat, you say?'

The last speaker detached himself from the group as they returned, laughing, to their dice-play, and came over to 'm Fega. He was a lean fellow with a foolish expression, but his eyes burned with intent.

'Wajlat?' he repeated.

'I serve 'l Saqi, the mining engineer,' said 'm Fega. 'He has made his fortune three times over, and I am proud to serve him, for it is well-known that an honest servant may rise to a respected position better than that of any hired labourer.'

'Honesty is a convenience, I am sure,' said the fellow with the burning eyes. 'And I am no hired labourer, but a skilled carpenter from Wajlat who has made his own fortune fitting cabins to the merchant ships being built here.'

'Wajlat,' said 'm Fega. 'Well, you may save your breath, for I have no other news of Wajlat, which I am sure is a place as wild as the human creatures who may be encountered there.'

And he looked the man up and down in contempt.

'Save your scorn,' said the man. 'I have good connections in Wajlat. Now tell me. Your freak, who it appears will be your new master: how old is he?'

'How should I know how old he is?' replied 'm Fega. 'At any rate he is still a boy, if he is not a demon. About eleven or twelve.'

'And his deformity?' persisted the man with the burning eyes. 'Is it . . .?' And he made movements with his hand across his chest to indicate the details of his question.

'm Fega started.

'How do you know this?' he asked. 'You have been talking to other servants of my master.'

'Not at all,' was the reply. 'I know what I know, and I know things that I have a good right to know.'

'There are many things which it is common sense to know,' said 'm Fega. 'And one of them is that a man should mind his own business, and not interfere in that of others.'

'And another is that it is not right that a freak should be in a position to inherit three fortunes at once,' said the man with the burning eyes. 'Particularly if he has been stolen in the first place.'

'Stolen, you say?' laughed 'm Fega. 'The forests of Wajlat belong to the Akond, and my master's fortunes were built on his loyal service to the Akond in the mines and engineering works constructed by him, and in the rubies extracted from those mines, the Akond's share duly accounted for. A man of 'l Saqi's standing, contracted to the Akond for many long years, may surely spear a boar or gather fungus in the forest where he is employed? Or any wild creature found running there? 'l Saqi certainly believes so, and he is a prudent man.'

'Prudence in one's affairs', said the man with the burning eyes, 'is often a means of better protecting them. In any case, what belongs to the Akond may belong to the Akond in more ways than you can know. I know what I know right enough, but you may not know what you know, or not know it rightly.'

'Come, man,' said 'm Fega angrily. 'You speak threateningly in riddles.'

'Peace, sir, I mean no harm,' said the man. 'In fact, I can be the means to do you more good than you could hope for.'

'What can you possibly know, that I do not know, that can do me good?' demanded 'm Fega.

'Be assured that I can solve your problem,' said the man, putting his hand for a moment on 'm Fega's sleeve, and smiling reassuringly.

'm Fega looked down at the man's hand, which was missing its first two fingers, and knew him for a scoundrel of some sort. None the less he was intrigued by the man's veiled speech and manner, and invited him to continue.

'If, as I heard you say at the beginning,' went on 'm Ezla (for it was he), 'your life will be easier when your master dies and you may, through the deformity, better control his estate for your own uses, how much better it would be for you if the deformity were to disappear as well?'

'Better indeed, so long as I were not charged with his murder!' said 'm Fega.

'm Ezla looked at him and smiled.

'Do you think it possible that we might come to an understanding in this matter?' he said.

'Do I understand you to be a rogue?' said 'm Fega.

'They say that it takes one to know one,' replied 'm Ezla. And his laugh was like the sound of the plane as it smoothes the timber of the gallows.

13

GOOD fortune is beautiful, like the concurrence of stars in their courses, but what are we to say of the good fortune of the wicked? Is it mere luck, for which there will be a price to pay? In stories it may be so, for it is in stories that we seek justice; in the world the mean-minded may continue to prosper, as a cracked calabash will leak unnoticed into the sand.

It was lucky for 'm Ezla that at this time the impresario 'm Baz came to the harbour seeking a team of carpenters to construct a great stage in the courtyard of the palace. The palanquin-boys shouted, the beggars scattered, and a great perfume rose in the air.

Despite his bulk, 'm Baz had the delicate gestures of the tiniest of birds. He dabbed his little finger at random in the direction of the carpenters who had clustered on the dock, and almost as soon as he had arrived, he was gone. The carpenters were taken in a wagon to the palace, with the wood following.

The Wazir acted in close consultation with 'm Baz

as the stage was erected, so that 'm Ezla feared recognition and worked with a scarf over his head, as if against the heat of the sun. And he watched for an opportunity to speak with 'm Baz alone.

He feared that the work would be completed and the carpenters paid and returned to Taflat before that opportunity came, but at last the Wazir retired and 'm Baz was to be found at the rear of the structure, nodding with satisfaction at the completion of the inner platform.

The bargain, such as it was, was as secure as may be between two opportunists. For 'm Baz prided himself on his menagerie of freaks of nature, both animal and human, which toured the villages to much amazement and the accumulation of small coins, and it was always in need of novelty. His eagerness to acquire 'l Isilik, when described to him, was not perhaps as great as 'm Fega's eagerness to be rid of him, but together their desires concentrated in 'm Ezla the perfect opportunity to tie a profitable knot. And in his mind was also a kind of revenge, for had he not come to the palace years before with an extravagant wish to reveal good news? And hadn't the Akond refused to hear him, and the Wazir decreed a cruel punishment? He had dimly understood then that his good news was not necessarily good news. Well then, there was nothing for it but that the angel cast out of heaven must be further cast down into the pit. There could be no half way. From the gleaming marble of the palace balcony and the acclamation of the crowds to the foul wicker of a freak menagerie and the hooting of the crowds, this was to be the fate of the Akond's first-born.

The Akond himself was in his element as the generous provider of entertainments. The chamberlain had unrolled and aired the best carpets, the court musicians had polished and re-tuned their instruments three-quarters of a tone sharp as had for centuries been the custom at the grandest banquets in order to imitate the sound of the victorious clarion, and the court itself had assembled entirely in white robes. The hangings of the banqueting-hall were white, the decorations were the fragile blossom of fruit trees, the platters all of ivory. Only the faded and patched relics of the uniforms of the French party, threadbare ultramarine and tattered crimson-and-gold, lent a touch of colour, like traces of ink and wax on an old document.

The musicians warbled and the first dish of the banquet was brought in to the accompaniment of bright arpeggios of melancholy delight, that to the ears of Colonel Marzipol, Captain Debussy and Captain Orqueban sounded like the squealing of bagpipes.

The Akond's cook had spent a week preparing the dish, an ancient ceremonial tradition usually reserved for weddings called 'The Creation of the World'. He had used up the entire octopus from Muscat simply to make the broth that was the basis of the dish. Little charcoal-burners were lit beneath the vast tureen to keep a friendly bubbling in the rich reduction of onion, marsh-fungus, harbour sprats, sea-jellies and the pulverised eight-footed monster which lent to the broth its own encouraging tinct of midnight magenta.

Into this nourishing essence the attendants freely cast, like husbandmen, the various seeds and eggs that gave the dish its lively name. But the effect of the dish was achieved as much through the deceiving art of the court conjuror as it was through the gastro-nomic ingenuity of the cook.

In a bowl of it presented with great good humour to Colonel Marzipol, he saw, staring rapt into its depths, the following: beans sprouting, the eggs of the tiniest nectar-gathering birds cracking and hatching into the seething fluid, yolk acquiring brief feathers, spawn flirting the ghosts of tails, embryos appearing to smile as in the grateful heat of the hammam, womb blood trickling and clotting into suggestive shapes, grains flowering, litter unfolding tender limbs as if to swim up to the spoon, leaves fanning, and a tiny tricolour in Japanese paper.

'A miracle!' exclaimed the Colonel.

The two captains were presented with their bowls, which they probed suspiciously with their porcelain spoons. Others cautiously lifted the scalding fecund liquid to their lips after seeing the Akond do so, but Anic waved his away. He was reserving his energy for goat.

'You may be interested to know', said Colonel Marzipol, 'that in my country it is becoming fashionable to eat in this way through creation. The Russians started it, but they are a race full of drama and surprises. You begin like this in the ocean, proceed to the animals that live on dry land and then to those that inhabit the air. Ambrosia is reserved for dessert.'

The schoolmaster, who was again present, and who had just burned his lips, offered a translation, but came to partial grief at the last sentence.

'Were the angels to condescend to visit my

humble palace', said the Akond, 'they would be assured of an appropriate welcome. But how would we know what to serve them? I suspect that they do not need to eat at all.'

The schoolmaster obliged again, and the two captains looked at each other, each thinking that if this was what their host knew he should serve them, then he did not know very much.

But their assumption was to receive a correction of sorts. After the obligatory goat (of which, to Anic's fury, they were exclusively offered the eyeballs), some frizzled fripperies of fish, some fruits and sherbets, a footman entered with a smaller platter which was placed directly in front of Colonel Marzipol and his fellow officers.

On this platter was a small grey disc.

At first the Colonel thought that it might be a sponge, and that he was being invited to wipe his fingers and mop his brow. But the disc was dry, and smelled strongly of something which, though disagreeable, was hauntingly familiar yet distant, like those aromas that can ambush us with lost memories of youth. The Colonel leaned forward to sniff, then smiled and looked around at the company. He brushed up his moustache, first to one cheek and then to the other, with the knuckle of his forefinger.

It was a Camembert.

'You will have to tell us how to eat it, this delicacy of your country,' said the Akond. 'It was difficult to obtain.'

Colonel Marzipol ceremoniously broached the shrunken cheese. He was obliged, rather than cut it vertically, to lever it open in its layers of grey and sooty yellow as though he were unpicking the cover of an old book. It could then be broken into small flakes.

'Utterly delicious,' said the Colonel.

For some reason there came into his head some old verses from his childhood that his grandfather used to recite to him:

'Think of the vole in the church of cheese:
Piety kept her on her knees,
But she nibbled the pews and gnawed the font
And munched all the hassocks that she could
     want.
"The Bishop" said she "will give me
     immunity,
Since a church isn't cheese but a vital
     community,

And God will appear on a hill, in a hole,
To a squadron of geese or a singular vole,
For He is merely the rare occasion
For a glimpse of truth like an equation."
But still she chewed from chancel to nave,
Altar and aisle and architrave,
For who would exchange a Camembert
For the mathematics of d'Alembert?'

While all this was going on, at the rear of the stage erected in the courtyard 'm Baz was lying on his back being made up as an elephant. He was already in bulk somewhat like an elephant, his shoulders, arms and enormous paunch grey with body hair, his small eyes set slightly to the sides of his heavy head. His fellow actor had covered 'm Baz's face and neck with turquoise, and was gluing on a concertina'd tube of wired cloth of the same colour. The make-up would soon be completed with a goggling frown in lines of red and black, and a pair of paper tusks.

Although this was to be a comedy, the elephant had a fierce appearance and a regal manner. The second actor was in turn painted with the fastidious mouth and astonished brows of a camel. The only concession to animal features was a pair of ears affixed to the head-dress. The camel was otherwise in female costume.

When the Akond and his company had taken their seats on the upper shaded balconies of the courtyard, the performance began. Captain Debussy, whose father was a Parisian lawyer, had often been to the Comédie Française, and took his seat in the vague expectation of something like Beaumarchais (if perhaps a little mistreated and indigestible, like the Camembert). Captain Orqueban had something more like Guignol in mind, for that was the popular entertainment of his Provençal village. Colonel Marzipol, who had read his *Arabian Nights*, hoped for a tale of the dangers of love, with fantastical adventures, and the theatrical effect of a magical carpet included.

None were prepared for the drum-accompanied dialogue of two howling and stamping, shin-greaved and skirted animals, who circled about each other in derision, striking postures of mock-submission and precarious triumph, wielding fans and maces, gargling and growling, jumping, crooning, wiggling eyebrows, fluttering tongues, batting eyelashes and spitting curses.

This went on for two and a half hours, heard in

attentive silence by the Akond's court and its guests, save for polite laughter and the occasional clatter of date stones on the marble and some helpful whispering from the Akond to the schoolmaster, and from the schoolmaster to Colonel Marzipol: 'This is the most celebrated play of the Camel and the Elephant. . . . the Elephant scorns the Camel as the servant of dry places. . . the Camel is the whore of the desert. . . the Camel has eaten all her children. . . the Elephant believes that he has become a god . . .'

The Colonel shifted uneasily on his hams.

'. . . the Camel is in a fury. . . the Elephant lives in a swamp and bathes himself in filth . . . if the Elephant is a god, then excrement is a god . . . there is only one god and Mahomet is his prophet . . .'

Captain Orqueban considered pretending to faint, so that he could be carried out by Captain Debussy.

'. . . now the Elephant is singing a hymn of praise to all the gods in turn . . . now the Camel is dancing the dance of the water of the oasis . . . now the Elephant is singing the song of the great rivers . . . now the Camel is dancing before Allah . . .'

Captain Debussy nodded, breathing heavily, and was woken by a dig from his Colonel's sharp elbow.

'. . . both animals deny being animals at all . . . the

Camel recounts the tricks she has successfully played on the Elephant . . . the Elephant recounts his military service with the Mughal Emperors . . . there will be a brief interval soon.'

At this last piece of information Colonel Marzipol brightened considerably, and even managed to whisper back a question to the Akond, who eagerly replied during the interval:

'Yes, of course, as well as being an uproarious comedy, providing the greatest role for our greatest actor, 'm Baz, it is also a serious paradigm of our national identity. Our country lies, you see, between Mahomet and Brahma, between the camel and the elephant. We lie on the periphery of belief, and on the periphery of empires. You might say that we are at the centre of peripheries, where freedom is nourished; at the focus of the unusual, where romance is an instinct. Fought over once, abandoned as intractable, refusing a choice of absolutes.'

'Can this be wise?' ventured Colonel Marzipol, thinking of Poland. 'How can you retain your independence?'

'By abandoning arms!' declared the Akond. 'Since we have no army, no one thinks it possibly worth attacking us.'

'If the empires on either side of you are powerful,' asked Colonel Marzipol, 'do you not have to take account of them? Do you not have to play your hand? A field lying between a road and a marsh will more easily become part of the marsh than the road.'

The Akond clapped his hands in delight.

'Of course, of course!' he said. 'And if it were truly so, then we should need to have a sense of our direction in order not to stagnate, but the great empires are now highly developed and diversified. Think not of a field lying between a road and a marsh, but a field lying between two meadows: on each side the rich pastures support their own livestock, which have no need to stray, since there is little to stray for. The merest butterfly would soon feel itself lost. But the small creatures of the field feel all the benefits of the pastures on either side; it is a place where the utterly different pollens may germinate freely. We have the best of both worlds, through our more objective understanding of them.'

'Hence the satirical comedy of the Camel and the Elephant,' concluded Colonel Marzipol. 'They are both beasts of burden who seem to be getting a little above themselves, are they not?'

'Precisely,' said the Akond. 'Slaves to their nature,

and therefore unfree. Slaves to their gods, and therefore unfree. True freedom lies in reason. But shall we
return for the second part of the performance?'

'Gladly,' lied Colonel Marzipol, for though he was
himself an active foot-soldier in the most modern
Empire of Reason, he did not look forward with
much relish to a further two or more hours of the
puritanical Camel and the epicene Elephant. For
what reason at all could be found between the hump
and the trombe?

14

BY THE custom which uz-Mabmabla so respected, it was she who was in charge of the training of Ahraz.

The dark innermost chambers of the women's apartments, hung with scarlet and maroon tapestries depicting royal seductions and the metamorphoses of snakes and tigers, were lit with the slightest of curling tapers whose special fragrance forbade entry. Servants brought towels and ewers to the door, but came no further. Children were banished.

At first it was barely necessary that Ahraz's body should be shaved, but shaved it was, with steel as fine as feathers, the gentlest of kisses against the skin. And then it was oiled daily, with a variety of oils designed to discover which were the most suitable for drawing out the sheen of the belly and the elasticity of the limbs. The fruit oils and flower oils were the most delicate, designed to soften and shadow the most hidden parts in textures of pearl and petal. Over most of her body, smoothed in by the giant hands of the eunuchs, the oil of almonds was sufficient.

A Tale

It was poured in a thin trickle from a porcelain spout into the little hollow between her shoulder-blades, and from there spread out over her shoulders and down her ribs with deep but gentle motions of the fingers. She lay across the knees of one eunuch while this was done, utterly relaxed as she had learned to become, her eyelids closed, like singed butterflies settled on her face, her thoughts far away. It felt as though she were being carried through the air.

The other eunuch sat facing the first, knee to knee, ready to receive Ahraz's body as it was rolled over towards him. He in turn lifted the jug high over her and allowed the oil to seep on to her small breasts. His hand covered the breasts and spread the little puddle with a slow circular motion moving outwards to each arm, which he lifted in turn, oiling the armpit, clutching and kneading the shoulder and bringing the thin residual veil of oil slowly up the arm to the elbow. As the motions of the hand came near to the elbow itself, her forearm, which hung down over the eunuch's black knuckles, moved up and down to the motions of his hand, and then remained for a while vertical, save for the flopped wrist, while the eunuch oiled it, his fingers and thumb just touching around the fragile thinness of the limb, and finally pinching the palm gently before release.

The body was again rolled over, back over the knees to the lap of the first eunuch, where Ahraz was once again prone. Oil was dribbled into the downy gully of her spine and swept back over the twin globes that covered the main hinge of her body, swept over and around till they glistened, like temples in moonlight. Another drop, and another, in the same place, and the globes were slightly parted to allow a black finger to insinuate the oil into the cleft between them, with a final flourish at the tiny wrinkled button that was hidden there.

Back across the knees, like something being carefully unwrapped, and the oil circled the belly lower and lower until it enriched those equal secrets beneath it. Here, where the entrance of generation lay suspended were films of skin which responded to oil with transformations of texture and tone – mothwing, elfskin, dewlip – trembling to convey sensation. Deeper insinuations of the attentive fingers were forbidden. They moved without significant pause down to the surprising convexity of the thighs and the little apples of the knee. Rolled over again, the legs offered the blind creases behind the knee for particular saturation, the prop of the calf and the small bony triangulation of ankle and heel. It was the sole of the foot that always required the greatest drenching and kneading, for this skin could never escape the whole weight of the body, however light the stance or step, and was always slightly shiny and discoloured.

Uz-Mabmabla supervised these rituals with the diligence that was required of her. It brought to her mind the flame of her own body in youth, and she often sadly hummed the tune of the old song:

'The flower of my body will blossom no more,
　　Not as before.
The milk of my body has dried in its bed,
　　Not as before.
The fruit of my loins is cold at its core,
　　Not as before.
The sap of my being is sunk in its stem,
　　Not as before.
And yet my skin is alive not dead,
　　But not for ever.
And my heart runs still with its drumming tide,
　　But not for ever.
And feels the force that is locked inside,
　　But not for ever.
The flash of the flint, the light from the gem.'

When uz-Mabmabla had danced in her youth, she had been instructed by the great uz-Qalassia, whose performance had so startled her Akond that he had collapsed and died on the spot. Juliba had been taught by uz-Luba, with modified effect. Should this process be taken further? Or did Blom, in the irritating self-protection of his passivity, deserve some stirring at his forthcoming rite of passage? He had as yet made no attempt to steal into the women's apartments, as was conventionally expected of his age and standing, despite its being severely forbidden. Anic's eldest son had already received, and boasted about, several thrashings, and Anic was as ridiculously proud of him as in-Blemim was secretly disappointed in Blom. Was it that Blom had no desire to be thrashed, or was it that he had no desire? If asked, he might have complained that he found it hard enough to do some of the things that were demanded of him, let alone do things that were forbidden. Why should they be forbidden if they were expected? He had been brought up to believe his father reasonable, and his father, for whom reason was a blessed light in the damp tunnel of life, was compelled to agree.

So, while the lithe and beautiful Ahraz was oiled

and drilled in her steps and gestures, Anic laughed in his brother's face.

'What are all the preparations for that we know are being conducted diligently in the secret places of the palace?' he asked defiantly. 'It's not blood that runs in the veins of your son, but milk. He was not fit for the First Gift, and will be even less fit for the Second Gift. Whoever begot him could not have been the son of my father, for I know that the red blood inherited from him fires me like wine, and my doings are those of a man.'

In-Blemim was angry, and struck his brother in the face.

'These are not things to be spoken to the Akond,' he said. 'Hold your peace.'

Anic held his peace.

But despite the blow, Anic's laughter left its shadow on his brother's face, and in-Blemim suffered even from Anic's silence. For Anic's part, he resolved to himself to prove the taint of weakness in the Akond's loins by going into Juliba and spending himself with her, as he had been used to doing with the servants of the palace. But how this was to be accomplished he did not know. It was known and accepted that after the production of an heir the

Akond was no longer to be received into the connubial bed, but Anic could not believe that his brother respected this peculiar tradition. Were not all these prohibitions designed simply to further the excitement of the chase of love? For anything to be forbidden, it must first be presumed that someone has an overwhelming desire for it. And must we not respond to our innermost desires? What is life about if it is not an expression of the mysterious forces that drive us to project our identities and to claim our physical share of the world? So Anic argued. But he did not see his way clearly. Juliba of the regal profile and distant manner, beloved of the wary Akond, was no easy fruit to be plucked from a garden wall.

The education of Ahraz continued. A week to the curling and pointing of each finger, while the court drummers rehearsed for her the underlying pattering narrative of the dance, seemed to her the only excuse for the vain attention to the exaltation of her body, for here was the understandable goal of language and story. In a parallel discipline of marital arts she was instructed in chess, for it was only in this game and in love-making that the intimate moments together of the young Akond and his consort were to be spent. All else was public ritual, or that delight in separation that derives from the thoughts of renewed union.

These exercises pleased her, as means to a precise end that had nothing to do with her feelings. It seemed miraculous that the angle of a wrist or the bending of a finger could express something like fear or large numbers or the passing of time. Or that the licensed movements of a small army of ivory could so formalise and direct the chances of conflict. In each case, the code could be worked for entirely fresh combinations, so that the possibilities in story or in game were endless. These stories and games were for the entertainment of the young Akond, as she well knew, but it was impossible that they should not also please her. As for love-making, in which she was also instructed, she could not tell whether it was likely to please her or not, for it was with other young girls of the palace that it was conducted and uz-Mabmabla was as precise, patient and reasonable in her demonstration with finger and tongue as she was with pawn and bishop. The rules and their variations were in each case the elaborate means to a single end, that of beauty in diversity, and the illusion of an infinite postponement of defeat. And even the exhibition of pleasure was accurately regulated and part of the performance.

In her own private chamber, at some perfectly natural moment such as the crisp biting of an apple, Ahraz was suddenly brought to remembrance of herself as a person, and of the experiences of her childhood, which were all she had. She wept for her father, 'l Cara, who was as good as dead to her, and she wept for her mother, who was truly dead and now hardly remembered.

And sometimes she thought of the strange shrouded boy that she had watched from the secrecy of her garden at Taflat. Was Blom as beautiful as he was? Surely Blom would be noble and eloquent, finding no difficulty in understanding and speaking? And kind, too, as her neighbouring boy had seemed kind, always sheltering some poor struggling creature beneath his burnous?

Whenever she looked out of the window of her confinement it was in hopes of seeing the young Akond that she was to marry, but only once did she catch sight of him, and that was at too great a distance for appraisal. What she did see were the fountains of the palace, like the fountain of 'l Saqi's house, but more elaborate, rank upon rank of them. Water in the centre of a house is like a sacred source, but these were a form of ostentation.

They looked to be escaping, with a beating of wings. They were like a ghostly eruption, a final scare fluttering into a drizzling mist.

But she knew that they were tethered at their base in their brimming pool by hidden pipes which blew them into their gulping, drenched existence. They were like statues that you might put your hand through, monuments that you could turn off: nothing much.

But for so long as they moved, they enlarged their space with a melancholy kind of stillness, a restlessness of infinite collapse.

15

MARZIPOL and Orqueban, naked save for borrowed drawers, entered the dank tunnel that led to the bathhouse.

'We are foolish to have come to the city,' said Orqueban, 'when everything at the palace is clean and at our disposal.'

'We should demonstrate our independence, I think,' said his colonel. 'We may not be welcome as the Akond's guests for ever.'

'Who can tell?' said Orqueban. 'What about the Turk Osman who has been here half his life?'

'Osman is, you might put it, the Turkish Resident here,' replied Marzipol. 'I guess that he is in the pay of the Porte and must send back confidential reports through the Gulf. But it is also clear that he has been bribed by the Akond. He has been given a villa in Taflat, with exciting company, and as a result the Sultan is persuaded that the country is not worth the conquest.'

'And you hope for such a position?' laughed

Orqueban. 'You think that the Directoire will ever listen to us? Perhaps it is the exciting company you crave?'

There was some truth in this, for the slight spruce body of Colonel Marzipol harboured a sentimental and passionate disposition that sought even the flesh of corners and darkness, but craved more than ever in the weariness of his travels a settled love.

He laughed.

'Perhaps,' he said.

'Is that why you are learning the language?' persisted Orqueban. 'Are you acquiring the terms of gallantry? The nuances of domestic bargaining? The jargon of the acquisitive householder? You are as bad as Menou.'

'I have much larger horizons than Menou,' said Marzipol.

For the moment, his immediate horizon was a damp stone wall illuminated by a flickering oil lamp, with dark alcoves and indistinct movements of human shapes.

'Well,' said Orqueban. 'Here is company of a sort. I hope you did not expect women.'

'Sodomites,' said Marzipol. 'And precious little water.'

In the public area there was a shallow pool heated by charcoal fires in conduits beneath. Steam enveloped the bodies seated around it or lying on its rim, as water was ladled directly on to hot stones. An old man whose tangled beard and hair covered his bare shoulders like a shawl stood mindlessly in the middle of it, urine dripping from his withered manhood unnoticed, like wine from the spigot of a distracted inn-keeper.

'Do you intend to step into that?' asked Orqueban.

'As willingly as into my death-bed,' replied Marzipol.

He laughed briefly, and into his head came the monitory words of the poet, verses known as a child and the refrain often on the lips of his grandmother:

> 'Breaking the skin of the water
> But keeping your own skin whole,
> Making waves, but aware of dissolution:
>   Care and caution make long life.
>
> Treading the finest lawns
> And keeping upright above them,
> Walking tall, but aware of dust:
>   Care and caution make long life.

Struck the flint in the brushwood
But keeping your fingers from burning,
The heart afire, but aware of destruction:
　　Care and caution make long life.'

He had not always been cautious, he reflected, and sometimes that had given him his greatest opportunities.

They sat on a stone bench at the wall of the chamber and looked in vain for someone who might be taking orders for a drink.

'Look,' said Orqueban. 'Isn't that our friend the Elephant?'

He pointed out a prone heap of flesh on the bench against the opposite wall being massaged by a black servant of the bath-house.

'The size is the same,' said Marzipol. 'And the hair. And the unusual breasts. But that evil fellow whispering in his ear is not, I think, our friend the Camel.'

'I rather hope', said Orqueban, 'that we are not observed.'

They were not observed, at least not by the elephantine impresario and his companion, who gripped his arm with an unembarrassed two-fingered hand. Nor could they, in that dark place of sighs, grunts and foetid exhalations, hear anything that was being said.

Whatever was being said seemed to involve the urging of the Two-Fingered Hand and the idle assent of the Elephant, with nods and the occasional revolve of the wrist. It was a masterful show of indifference, designed to limit a vaguely promised disbursement, on the part of the Elephant. For Two-Fingers it was the rightful claim of a contract. Weariness met ingenuous certainty with the purpose of reducing the agreed sum, and between each exchange the fists of the masseur thundered on the Elephant's hairy shoulders like punctuation.

These were minor details in the immediate fate of the boy 'l Isilik, whose name had now, had he but thought of it, acquired a new depth of meaning. From being known he was lost and became unknown, and from being found he became known, and named, whereupon he was stolen and became again unknown, and again lost. He was dimly aware that these processes all involved entrapment of sorts, but what would the entrapment lead to?

On the morning when he took 'l Saqi's frail hand in his own two and found no response and saw it fall back on to the bed-sheet like an object dropped by accident, he knew that his own future was in peril. The hand had grown weaker and weaker, but so long as it fell back on the sheet in the shroud of its own weariness, the forefinger still just slightly raised as if there were something more to say, 'l Isilik knew that another day would go forward in which he could care for the old man, and supervise his comforts. Even if 'l Saqi's eyes were closed, 'm Fega would still bow before the bed and do 'l Isilik's bidding, but the boy knew that it could not last. And it did not last. When 'l Saqi was seen to be cold there was nothing to prevent the seizing of his keys, and after the seizing of the keys there was nothing to prevent the seizing of 'l Isilik.

He was put in a large cage of wicker, little more than a laundry basket, and taken to the cellar. The machinery of his supposed kidnapping by 'm Ezla was crudely performed, but was reckoned likely to deceive the lawyers who might (or might not, indeed) investigate the absence of a named heir. It would be presumed that the boy had fled in panic, with a significant box of rubies, on the death of his eccentric patron. Surprise would be expressed that 'l Isilik had been named as 'l Saqi's heir. Who could have known of this? No one knew! Least of all the boy, who could barely talk and was little more than an animal. It was all an old man's sentimental fantasy, ridiculous when you think that the object of his unnatural affection turned out to be nothing more than a common thief.

The gate was unlocked, and 'm Fega retired to bed. He had received his money in advance from 'm Ezla, but money was not an issue. With 'l Isilik out of the way, he had full access to 'l Saqi's riches and that was more than enough. 'm Ezla came in the night to the cellar, barely more than a lean and knotted shadow on the wall, and took 'l Isilik. Nothing was heard at the time, and 'm Fega was happy to think no more about either of them.

And who indeed was there to think about 'l Isilik now? To be alone is not necessarily to be lonely, for if you are conscious of the possibility of being thought about, then the spirit reaches out effortlessly to others. So, beautifully, the very thinking of them creates the necessary bond. Think of someone thinking of you, and it animates the memory of them at the centre of your own needs. You have captured them for your own purposes, which is to know, sometimes against all odds, how they might respond to your demands, were they to be present in the body. And this in turn helps to define what those demands might be.

'l Isilik had no one but Ahraz.

This was the neighbouring girl to whom he had only spoken from an inaudible distance, and to whom he had spoken not words but projections of his idea of her as a solitary waif in her tree. He had thought her perfect face in the foliage like a ruby among emeralds, expressing a power in light and colour that was identical to nature's, and merely weaker in the leaf than in the blood. Or like a trick of his dreams of her, where red achieved an identity with green.

Then she had been taken away, and her tree was empty, like a summer nest. Suppose that her father had gone, and she had stayed. There might, he vaguely thought, have been a natural union of their two houses, a melting of the neighbouring frost between merchant and engineer. Perhaps it was because she had been taken that he had been taken also? For he had no idea, either where she had gone or where he himself now was. A blanket had been flung over his cage, a perpetual night. The crudest provisions were occasionally thrust inside for him, and he was forced to relieve himself where he squatted.

And after days of this, 'l Isilik found himself emitting sounds that he had not heard since he had first begun to mouth real words at 'l Saqi's fatherly insistence, old bestial sounds that belonged to darkness and to primitive requirements, wolfish sounds that now made him ashamed, much more ashamed than he was of his own dirt and his own smell.

And then he remembered the verses that he loved to learn at 'l Saqi's knee, and he tried to recapture their comfortable sounds and shapes. What was it? 'The space with no name'? No. 'The face with no space'? No, that wasn't it either, but both made sense to him in his present plight. What he needed was certainly a face, and the face that he desired and which just eluded him was the face from its neighbouring tree.

'O Ahraz, where are you? Do you remember an eye at the chink in your garden wall? Do you remember plaiting rushes for a fan to cool your father in his stunned and sullen stillness on the verandah? Do you remember your garden song? Are you grown into a woman yet?

'I clutch between my own arms something like an image of my death, which I now daily expect.'

16

THE APPEARANCE of the ragged platoon of the French had pleased no one so much as Blom, not least because it diverted the attention of the court from the widely perceived problem of getting him into a fit state for the receiving of the Second Gift. To be observed, continually if sometimes secretly, is a hazard of princehood which only the most self-assured can tolerate. Blom knew that he was a disappointment, and therefore was extremely sensitive to the critical eyes he found about him in every chamber, watching from corners, bowing ironically, tasting his food, proposing fresh jokes and indulgences, leading away yet again the unwanted horse.

But the great novelty of entertaining Colonel Marzipol and his men provided a stir of gossip, a rush of unwonted activity, and a redirection of servants, within which the young Akond could once again, as in childhood, find himself partly invisible. And he enjoyed playing chess with Colonel Marzipol, who did not treat him as anything other than a worthy opponent, and was now able to converse, if haltingly, in his language.

'Your turn,' said the Colonel, having pushed his king's pawn forward two squares.

'You are supposed to say "your Exaltedness", you know,' said Blom.

'I am?' asked the Colonel. 'Well, I certainly don't want you to call me "Colonel". Perhaps we could dispense with formalities. After all, I am not one of your subjects. And come to think of it, nobody is – yet. They are your father's subjects, aren't they?'

Blom found this refreshing. He was very used either to sniggering deference or calculating rudeness from palace officials, while what he disliked most of all was the craven flattery of self-advancement. There was no one he could trust.

He did not particularly trust Colonel Marzipol either, but felt secure in a relationship with him that seemed more open than any other.

He moved his own king's pawn two squares. And immediately Colonel Marzipol moved his king's bishop's pawn two squares.

'Why,' exclaimed Blom, 'I can take the pawn!'

He thought perhaps that Marzipol was humouring him and allowing him to win. He took the pawn, and again without pause Marzipol brought out his king's knight to the square in front of the young Akond's advanced and isolated pawn.

'You are not one of my subjects indeed,' said Blom, 'but I suspect that you are patronising me.'

Marzipol raised the eyebrows that were like trim circumflex accents over his wide and innocent eyes.

'You have not come across this opening before?' he asked, 'It is a common gambit, one of the oldest. See: my development is perfectly sound so far, and you have only one pawn in play, and that precariously, as on the edge of a cliff.'

'I must protect it,' said Blom, moving up his king's knight's pawn two squares in support. 'You see,' he went on, 'Ininin the Wazir lets me win. At least he can't be so bad a player as he seems to be, giving me pieces at crucial moments. He wants to keep in my favour.'

'To preserve his own position when you become the Akond, I take it?' said Marzipol. 'In case you wish to appoint one of your friends?'

'Yes,' said Blom, doubtfully. 'Except that I don't have any friends.'

'I am your friend,' said Colonel Marzipol.

Blom laughed.

'But *you* couldn't be my Wazir,' he said.

'Why not?'

'I'm not sure.'

Blom was embarrassed, and looked down at the board. Marzipol had moved out his white bishop to the queen's bishop's fourth square, so he decided to develop his own black bishop on the adjacent diagonal by moving it in front of his knight.

'Do you want to be the Akond?' asked the Colonel.

'It may be much better than being what I am now, which is neither one thing nor the other,' said Blom. 'I would rather be a pet cat than be what I am now.'

'How so?' asked Marzipol, moving his king's rook's pawn forward two squares.

'A pet cat not only enters or leaves a room totally as it pleases,' said Blom, 'but it has no idea if it is noticed or not. That is what I would like. To be entirely unconcerned about being seen.'

'Do you think servants are happy?' asked Marzipol.

'They'd be noticed if they weren't where they were meant to be, or not doing what they were supposed to do. So they must always be anxious, as I am.'

'But not animals?'

'They have nothing to do but please themselves.'

Blom was staring at the Colonel's last move.

'Does this move please *you*?' he asked. 'I suppose it must, if you've played it.'

'It is recommended by the great Philidor,' said Marzipol, 'whom I once had the honour of playing at the Café de la Régence before the war.'

'It leaves your king half-naked,' said Blom. 'For once again I can take the offered pawn.'

'Of course,' said the Colonel. 'And I may recapture. But it is the file of the bishop which is weak for you. You will be tempted to attack the rook's file, but you had better beware.'

'You are telling me your secrets,' frowned Blom. 'Did Philidor advise this too?'

'I am your guest and your friend,' said Marzipol. 'And if we talk about the moves I shall be free with you. What, shall I treat you like a pet cat to be ignored while I lay down some trap?'

Were they indeed traps, these amiable lingerings and civilities of the French? Debussy was free with his drugs, which induced obligations. Colenso had taken a small house in Taflat, and a plump bride to go with it. Many had acquired elements of the language, though none with the astonishing proficiency of Colonel Marzipol. What did all this mean? It might, of course, have meant that it was the French themselves who were trapped. But the Akond took it to mean that they had simply abandoned their original plans, always supposing that there ever had been such plans, and were happy for the foreseeable future to make their home in his kingdom.

He had, in any case, other things to think about. Since the quarrel with his brother he had been much troubled in his mind. He had always thought Anic harmless, as younger brothers conventionally present themselves; not very tractable, of course, but genuinely concerned with his own limited interests and presenting no threat. Now he was not so sure.

There were signs of real jealousy in his tiresome joking about Blom, as though any one of his own children had a better right to become Akond. He had never shown jealousy on his own account.

But all this seemed petty and theoretical to in-Blemim. Anic's feelings, even if they were truly felt and not mere theatre, could have no practical issue in the arrangements for Blom's inheritance. What he was most worried about was the attention paid by Anic to Juliba, which sometimes went beyond brotherly greeting or the tolerated compliments of palace life.

'Honoured sister,' Anic would intone, 'whose mocking mouth scatters the hopes of wretches, whose bearing and tread are the torture of rascals, whose eyes are fixed as the chaste moon above the fatal clouds where she must sail like –'

But even he, in the flushed comedy of his prating, could not summon the skill or effrontery to continue his metaphor. At another time, he ordered the palace musicians to appear after dinner and made them accompany his wavering tenor in an old courtly song of the poet, adapted by him with some petulant daubs and hatchings of irony:

> 'Well might she discreetly yawn
> Into the back of her hand,
> For vigil is our love's observance
> And the hours sand.
>
> Locked in her hair are light and fire.
> Locked in her skin is touch.
> But the soul that peeps from her tongue's
> chink
> Is nothing much.

Never was a longing that
Could steal by her unknowing
Or stir that great abundance to
    An overflowing.

Never was a jest she did not
Turn with a toss of the head
Into a stony epitaph
    On love unsaid.

Coolness might work with her, except
For fiery eyes that bear
Her folded sex before her like
    A silent prayer –'

'Enough!' exclaimed the Akond, dismissing the musicians. He had barely noticed the changes that Anic had made to the song, but he was aware that the listeners were uneasy.

On this and other similar occasions, the Akond was torn between roaring out his ill-humour and playing down the flirtation by ignoring it. He would shoo his brother away with backward motions of his hand, or take him gently by the shoulders, turning him around and propelling him towards the door. Anic would laugh in acknowledgement of the outrageousness of his own effusions, and sometimes even in-Blemim might smile a little, for at heart he was fond of his brother.

But on these occasions he would also notice a high colour in Juliba's cheek and a concern to appear unconcerned. And once, when they really thought themselves unobserved, he saw her dismiss the attentions of Anic's hand, which had laughingly touched hers, by thoughtlessly grasping it and putting it from her, as though it were an untrained animal whose familiarity she was wearily used to.

'Too hot!' thought in-Blemim. 'And at our advanced stage of life! Why, villains have lost fingers for presuming as much.'

17

JULIBA retreated more and more into the women's apartments, without excuse. And the Akond could not bring himself to follow her there, even though as the authority behind the law forbidding the entry of men he could easily have put it aside and entered. Even his brother had often done so, though not without some scandal.

There she could bathe and talk with the women of the palace as she pleased, and be free of the attentions of men.

The Akond rebuked her for her absences, complaining that he was often lonely in his private chamber. So she was moved to invent reasons for not visiting him, such as that uz-Luba had a fever and needed watching through the night.

'Let uz-Mabmabla do it,' he said, 'or some attendant woman who has no obligation to her husband.'

'So,' said Juliba, 'our love has turned cold because it has become an obligation, has it? I am not surprised, since at our first meeting I was obliged to dance for you. In all those years you have not been obliged to do anything that was not of your prior choosing. So do not speak to me of obligations.'

Juliba was herself shocked to hear these words leave her lips almost without her knowing that she had voiced them. She blushed deeply, and looked away from in-Blemim, noticing a strange crack in the wall shaped like the leg of a mantis. It reached to the doorway as if to destroy it. She returned immediately to the women's apartments.

It was evening, the hour when once upon a time musicians were accustomed to be summoned to the Akond's chamber to play music of celebration and longing for him and Juliba, when lamps would soon be lit, but not yet, and when incense rose in tranquil wisps to the ceiling. Without Juliba, the musicians were not summoned, and the lamps remained unlit. And the Akond sat for a long time alone in his slowly darkening chamber, trying to be aware of himself thinking to some purpose.

Juliba found Ahraz in one of the cushioned apartments, her training for the day accomplished, lying with her head in the lap of uz-Mabmabla, listening to her stories. Juliba quietly took up some sewing which she had earlier left there and settled down to listen herself.

'In the old days,' recited uz-Mabmabla, 'which are now so long ago that I cannot remember anyone who quite remembers them, we were a warlike nation. The Mughals came from the East and the Turks from the West, like arrows across a ravine. Instead of ducking our heads and allowing our enemies to fall upon each other without noticing us, which would have been the sensible thing to do, we summoned the flower of our youth and rode against each army in turn. Was this a mistake? It is impossible now to tell. If we had not fought, we would at some time or another have had to test our strength against those who conceived the desire to possess us. It would have been impossible to live in the continued expectation of such an attack. The need for perpetual readiness would have wearied us to weakness.'

Juliba looked up from the smaragdine stitches that would for ever define an uncurled summer leaf.

'What have women to do with such things?' she murmured.

Uz-Mabmabla smiled.

'You must remember that our service to men obliges them to protect us,' she said.

'Or is it that their valour obliges us to support them?' suggested Juliba.

'There is a difference, I suppose,' said uz-Mabmabla. 'And that is why we in turn must become the private moralists and chroniclers of their adventures. After all, if the Turks had been allowed to ride down the valley unhindered, it is us that they would have had in view. Gold, rubies, spice, the harbour at Taflat, all of interest to them in the aggrandisement of their empire, no doubt, not to mention the satisfaction of destroying our army, but to take the women and to make them bear Turkish children, that would have been their aim. That is how empires are achieved. Only the strength of our army, and the risks they took, shielded us from shame.

'Or so the story goes. In the event, we dealt with each enemy so cruelly that they have left us alone ever since. We took no prisoners, and did not allow them to bury their dead. Those janissaries who were able to flee took back accounts of the engagement that curdled the blood even of such hardened warriors as the Turks. The Turkish word for "nose-lessness" is to this very day a word borrowed from our language. Does this surprise you? It should, knowing the peace in which we live today.'

'It makes me ashamed,' said Juliba quietly.

'But it is not as if our army did not suffer,' continued uz-Mabmabla. 'It did. When our warriors rode out to meet the Mughal host and took their stand on the left bank of the river below Sarapa, they found themselves on the site of the earlier battle, where they had crossed over to encounter the Turks. The banks were still spongy with the piled corpses, preserved in mud, and when the attack was ordered the spurred cavalry flung up divots of mailed flesh and stumbled in the thickly bedded lances. Can you believe it? These were former comrades, still remembered two years on in drunken barrack reminiscence, legends in their time though their actual bodies were stretched to the vultures and seeded with rushes. Yes, it makes me shudder, too.

'The Akond of the time felt the disgust of his warriors keenly. He hated to lose so many men in the course of turning back invader after invader, and he hated even more making them into such remorseless fighting machines. So he made a decision to disband the army, whatever the cost to the future security of the country, retaining only a small élite cadre as a palace guard. These are the men you admire, Ahraz, when you gaze out of the window. Don't deny it!'

Ahraz could not summon the energy to deny it.

'They are perfectly trained and completely equipped,' continued uz-Mabmabla, 'but there are never more than fifty of them. Their lives are ceremony, though the old traditions are in their blood. We could, in an emergency, rely on their absolute service, but of course it would be of little use against a determined army.

'The disbanded legions, exultant in victory but ashamed in blood, were put to work on the land. Acres in the valley were planted with rice, the spice plantations extended, bee-hives constructed out of old suits of armour. The dusty earth was turned over with swords, and stock-fences constructed with lances. Irrigation pipes were laid from old cannon. Do soldiers make good farmers? I hardly think so. They are used to seeking a decisive outcome, and are too impatient to attend the seasons. Only a good general can direct a harvest as he would direct a battle; the foot-soldiers of the soil left to themselves became scavengers of their own husbandry. Their animals starved, and the crops failed.'

'Did they not themselves die?' asked Juliba.

'Sometimes,' said uz-Mabmabla. 'But to die of hunger on the land is not very different from dying of wounds. To survive, any man must contrive to match his own skills against an unknown force, and even in times of peace, nature can be an enemy, perhaps our worst. Life itself is a battle. The land must be cultivated with the far-sighted strategy and resourceful tactics of a great commander, which is why our spice plantations are in effect governed by a vast military machine, under the direction of uz-Blemim.'

All the time she narrated this history, uz-Mabmabla stroked Ahraz's forehead, smoothing back the strands of her dark hair, and Juliba from her corner listened to these accounts of the past with fresh interest, though she had heard them many times before, asking questions that she thought Ahraz might have wanted to ask if she had not been so drowsy. A thought occurred to her, and she spoke up again from the shadows where her fingers worked the needle furiously like the prow of a cutter in a storm.

'Nature wants us to die,' said Juliba.

Uz-Mabmabla looked across at her, and sighed.

'No woman could say such a thing', said uz-Mabmabla, 'who has not a stone for a heart.'

'It is true,' persisted Juliba. 'And women know its truth better than men do, for while men fear their own individual deaths, women fear the deaths of their children and therefore of all mankind.'

'It is noble to die in an honourable cause.'

'Is it noble to die in poverty?'

'It is noble to die in war.'

'Is it noble to die in peace?'

'Without death, we would overrun the earth.'

'Without death, we could understand the earth.'

'We learn our proper humility from death.'

'How, from breeding ranks for indiscriminate slaughter?'

'By knowing the limitations of our bodies.'

'The body behaves as though it is immortal, craving more and more satisfactions even when exhausted by them. We find ourselves unhappy with what we have, though the greatest blessings may be heaped upon us, and then we look vainly to create new or alternative lives for ourselves that can't fail to make us even more unhappy.'

'We must try to live virtuously.'

'I know that, but I also know that it is hard to do so.'

And a tear moved down Juliba's cheek like a finger silently reading her secret grief, and uz-Mabmabla saw something of its reflection in the lamplight. She again took up her role as the teacher of history's lessons.

'In the endless cycles of peace and war,' uz-Mabmabla continued, 'that afflict kingdoms, that between men and women is not the most grievous. But its engagements and truces are a model for all the others. Of all such human struggles the greatest is that between the old and the young. Societies that teach a respect for age know very well that such respect is not natural. The young hate the old for their collapsed appearance, their wealth and their power. Given a perfect freedom to do what they liked, the young would be happy to do away with the old. For their part, the old secretly hate the young for possessing a larger share of life and the promise of a future that they themselves will not know. Such jealousy can be so strong that for their part also the old would happily do away with the young. Are you surprised at this?

'What is it that prevents such a wholesale war between the generations? Only the desire of old men for young girls and a mother's love for her children, and don't such feelings often strike us as self-indulgent or foolish? In all other relationships between the old and the young it is never long before the hatred shows itself. It was like that after the disbanding of the army, for war is of course an effective means of killing off the young, and without it the old feel challenged by the new generations and will try new ways to keep them down. Can you imagine a kind of tribal feud, not between families, not between the sexes, but between the generations?

'I will not speak of the shameful hostilities that ensued, the flower of manhood pursued through the marshes by senile mobs, the infanticide, the smothering of grandmothers, the defacing of beauty by the impotent. A cure had to be found quickly for such chaos, or our nation would speedily die out.

'The answer, of course, is that the old need the young, and not only do the old need the young, they are also in a way still the young themselves, since having once been young, they forever contain youth. The same is not true of the young themselves, for they cannot imagine ever being old. So, to preserve the peace, the positions of authority must pass quickly to the relatively young, and no one must be allowed visibly to grow old. No Akond will willingly cling to power any longer than tradition now imposes; only twenty-one years will pass between his receipt of the Third Gift and his bestowing of it, so that the Akond is never old. Would that such a heartening system were extended in all walks of life throughout the kingdom!'

Juliba, whose unhappiness, though largely incomprehensible to her, was due in large part to a sense of her life running away with her too rapidly into a predictable dryness, shuddered.

'What a great deal of nonsense!' she murmured.

Ahraz was asleep.

18

IF, AS uz-Mabmabla claimed, no Akond was ever old, it was also true that no old Akond was ever really old. To fear death as the old Akond feared death was as much a response to the custom of the country and to the translations of royal status as it was a genuine terror based upon natural decline or the investigations of doctors.

'Too much thinking in this solitude has turned you into an old man before your time,' said in-Blemim to his father when he visited him again on the eve of the celebration of the Second Gift. 'You must live for each moment of life as it comes to you.'

'These moments that you speak of,' said the old Akond, 'what are they, exactly, that they come and go? Usually they are the responses of my body to circumstances over which I have little or no control. Is this the case, then, that I am nothing but the product of these arbitrary visitations? A series of states of being produced largely by accident or the uncaring actions of others? A context for experienced events that in themselves no longer exist and might just as well never have existed?'

'You are surely more than that,' protested in-Blemim. 'You are, after all, your sovereign self.'

Uz-Blemim looked at his son with some amusement.

'I am only a retired Akond,' he said, 'who feels that his life has passed too quickly. My "self", as you choose to put it, has been put at the disposal of my country and its traditions. I have hardly had the time to discover what my true self might be. Although I am very well aware of my suffering person.'

They were riding side by side on mules to Amora, the place in a temperate upper valley beyond Samsela that was the site of the old Akond's new Pleasure Dome. In-Blemim thought it quite absurd that someone who had recently built for himself such a place of indulgence should now be talking about suffering. He had hoped to persuade his father to return south with him on this occasion, so that he could witness the presentation to his grandson of the Second Gift and enjoy all the accompanying festivities. Finding him in such a gloomy mood made him all the more resolved to overcome his resistance to the journey, and to reunite him with uz-Mabmabla.

'What is suffering?' he asked his father. 'Is it not in your case merely an unreasonable fear of suffering?'

'I would ask you in turn what is reasonable or unreasonable,' replied the old Akond. 'Or, indeed, whether reason has anything at all to do with the matter. The poets have always told us that happiness only exists in the anticipation of happiness, and I do believe that to be true:

> "What is to come is most in our hearts,
>   The hope of a hand, the promise of meeting,
>   The sense of the strangeness that suddenly
>   starts
>   A joy in the prospect, the eager greeting
>   Of the friend who soon enough departs,
>   The eyes and the fingers, the words that are
>   fleeting."

We are fierce in our pursuit of the joys that we claim as our due, and take the greatest pleasure in looking forward to them. But whoever looks back on such happiness with equal pleasure? Can there be any pleasure at all in past happiness? It has, after all, gone for ever, and can never return. It might just as well never have existed. We even resent it for being over, and we are jealous of the present happiness of others. No, happiness most resides in its immediate prospect, and if that is the case then the same must be true of suffering. If suffering is to come, as it surely must, then it is our awareness of its inevitability that makes us most deeply suffer. Otherwise we would be mere animals, blissfully careless of what the future holds.'

At this, the old Akond's mule gave a great sneeze, as if to underline the point. Or was it an objection? After all, it was used to bearing its robed burden, and to feeling the whip, and had grown accustomed to associating these discomforts with the eventual provision of fodder. But it did not know that it would die.

'You are not at this moment', replied his son, 'the same person who will at some unspecified time of your life actually suffer. When that time does come, surely you may look back on yourself at this present time as a creature living in comparative, indeed in absolute, felicity? As you yourself have just said, the moment will have gone for ever and could not return. You will, in your time of suffering, regard it as the greatest perfection of your individuality, now lost to you, an unrecapturable state of being. If it will be so lost to you, so equally is your future state of being inaccessible to you now. There is no connection between them. Thus you will not then be the same person as you are now, and you are not now what you will become. Does this not relieve your anxiety?'

'No,' said the old Akond. 'And that must be because my mind is able to range freely over all these half-remembered and hypothetical states of being, and it is my mind and not my being that is anxious. I sometimes wish that I could extinguish my mind like the flame of a candle that is restless in an evening breeze, and yet leave my being whole, like the candle itself, and unconsumed.'

The Akond thought about this for a moment, and then said: 'I doubt that a candle is truly a candle at all if it is not giving light, and a man without a mind is merely an automaton. Or else a corpse.'

At length they came to Amora, and the Akond expected to see his father's Pleasure Dome.

'Where is it?' he asked, looking about him. They dismounted, and a servant took charge of the mules. A trivial stream moistened a declivity of rock and soon disappeared into a nibbled area of yellow grass. Further away were several thickets of solomon trees.

'Down here,' said the old Akond, leading his son

over the sward that was coloured by the freshet and across a slope that fell away to one side of it. 'Look.'

The Akond then saw some miscellaneous waist-high walls incompletely circling a pile of stone. Beyond them a half-buttress reached out into the empty air. At his feet was an elaborate pathway of cream and crimson marble that led up to the walls and then stopped.

'Why,' he exclaimed. 'It's a ruin!'

The old Akond laughed grimly.

'How can it possibly be a ruin', he said, 'when it is still incomplete?'

'I understood it to have been built,' replied his son. 'You have brought me up here to see a ruin.'

'I wish you wouldn't always be so bad-tempered,' said the old Akond. 'I thought you would be interested to see it. I never said that was finished.'

'I would indeed be interested to see it, but there is nothing to see.'

'Can you not imagine the whole?'

'I could imagine such a place in my bed at night with perfect ease. Here I am conscious only of the wildness of the situation and the dilapidation of the structure.'

'It is true that some stones that were once in place

have since fallen away, but that is no reason to call it a ruin. It is all still potential, and the buildings may be of infinite extension.'

'And yet you continually claim that your life is finite, and that its end inexorably approaches?'

The old Akond had no answer to this, but seemed much troubled by the paradox. He continued to lead his son over the site, and they looked down for some minutes at two workers who were digging out the chambers of an ice-house.

At length he replied: 'I suppose that when there is evidently something still to be done there is hope that there may be time to accomplish it.'

'That is true,' said in-Blemim. 'Otherwise we would venture on nothing in the fear that some accident might prevent us from taking it forward.'

The two labourers had thrown down their picks on seeing their master, and were grovelling in the stones. Uz-Blemim motioned to them to continue with their work.

'When you visited me seven years ago on the occasion of the First Gift,' he said, 'you told me that it was ridiculous to complain of having used up a third of my remaining portion of life when two-thirds still remained. Very soon, of course, that was no longer true, and it came about that I had used up exactly half of what remained. The odds on prospective pleasure and the expectation of existence had levelled. Now you come to me on the eve of the Second Gift, and the odds have shortened. I have only a third of that portion remaining, and your philosophical consolation no longer works. What remains to me continues to dwindle. And insofar as it remorselessly dwindles, the less can I believe in my own history. My continued existence adds to it every day, but I have no confidence in it. Where is it to be found? Where is the evidence that I have lived? And if the evidence is to be found somewhere, of what use is it to me? For that matter, of what use is it to anyone else? As you yourself pointed out, the evidence is easily misinterpreted. The Pleasure Dome is not yet finished, but a stranger passing by might conclude that it once had existed and had long fallen into disuse. In that case, would the sports and banquets he might imagine having taken place in it be any the less real than those that in fact have not yet taken place in it?'

'No,' replied in-Blemim. 'Nor would they be any more real.'

'But what of the similar pleasures that I have

experienced elsewhere?' asked his father. 'Are they any more real?'

'Of course,' said in-Blemim. 'If you experienced them, they are real.'

'And if there is no evidence of their having existed?'

'Of course.'

'And if I do not even remember them myself?'

'Even so.'

'Then I am truly puzzled,' concluded the old Akond. 'For then there may be all sorts of real events that no one knows about, doing goodness knows what mischief. I prefer to rely on what I may be certain about.'

'Do you remember that you have a grandchild?'

'I do indeed.'

'Then I suggest that you leave this place of purely hypothetical pleasure and return with me to the real world, where your grandson Blom is being prepared to receive the Second Gift. It will give you something to think about.'

They remounted their mules, and returned to the palace at Samira. The old Akond thought his son a bully, and the Akond thought his father a pathetic failure. But it was at last decided that uz-Blemim should travel south for the celebrations. Once there, the Akond thought, he might be persuaded for a time to be slightly happy.

19

IN THE temporary absence of the Akond, the Wazir Ininin had continued with the arrangements for the ceremony of the Second Gift, which was now close at hand. The chamberlain and the palace cook had been long instructed, and the conjuror had conferred with 'm Baz about the evening's entertainment. In deference to the interests of the young Akond and to his childhood fetish, the presentation of the Gift was to occur within a play that featured his shell, and there was to be both music and magic.

Anic summarily informed the Wazir that on the morning of the celebrations he would at last challenge Dibl to an encounter on the Field of the Goat, and that the whole court would assemble at Ormund to witness his certain success. Ininin bowed deeply, and dared not refuse the Akond's brother.

But Juliba, hearing the decision, let out a laugh before her discretion could reign it in. It was not a laugh of derision, nor of affection or concern. It was, rather, a laugh of surprise at her own feelings, and of a guilty recognition that Anic's gesture was made as much for her as for the hope of a reflected glory to fall on Blom. Since Blom had never shown the slightest interest in the Field of the Goat, the challenge, if successful, could only draw attention away from him and upon his uncle.

The laugh did not go unnoticed, and Anic contrived to come to Juliba privately.

'You think that I cannot prevail against the mighty Dibl?' he asked her, gripping her elbow.

The illicit touch nearly made her faint. It sent a tremor of the skin along her arm and down her back. Anic's face was near hers, and she could see the whorled grains of hair on his cheek springing afresh after the attentions of the morning razor, like the contrary patterns of storm clouds. She realised at that moment how long it had been since a man's hand had given her such feelings, and she shivered with foreboding.

'You think that I will not prevail?' repeated Anic.

'I don't know,' said Juliba weakly.

'Suppose that I win,' persisted Anic. 'You must acknowledge my prowess?'

'Yes,' said Juliba.

'And you will look favourably upon me?'

'Yes,' hesitated Juliba.

'And on my adoration of you?'

She was silent. His fingers still held her arm.

'Will you? Will you?'

She blushed, and nodded, and looked down at the floor, where a beetle, trapped by the hem of her garment, was struggling on its back, its legs moving in instinctive synchrony like the arms of a juggler.

Though each thought they were alone, Ahraz was behind a screen in the apartment, aghast at what she had overheard, and alarmed at her own involvement now that she had overheard it, she who was supposed for the time being to be invisible.

When the Akond returned from Samira with his father, everyone was shocked to see the old Akond at the palace and did not know if they were meant to feign an ignorance of who he was. Servants remembered past favours and misdeeds. Uz-Luba and uz-Mabmabla were stirred out of their long assumption of a fictitious mourning to greet him with the tentative embraces of estranged mother and deceived wife. They looked for the remembered man who had once played the role of Akond with perfect enthusiasm and propriety and saw only a lean simulacrum who was now playing the role of the old Akond with an equal if distracted formality. They soon retreated to the women's apartments to shed their tears. And Blom stared at his grandfather as though at a celebrated ancestor commemorated in a statue to be visited occasionally in a public place.

But Anic flung his arms around his father and clapped him on the back as though he were a victorious partner in the games, and talked to him of the small affairs of his life as though they had all occurred in the previous week and had only been missed by uz-Blemim through a brief and unexpected absence. His father stared at him with a dazed smile, unable to conceal his growing wonderment and affection.

When Anic's challenge to Dibl was revealed, the Akond was displeased. His reason might have warned him that his father would be more moved at a reunion with his younger son than at a meeting with the grandson whom he had never seen at all, but his jealousy of Anic overcame him, and he went to Ininin and criticised his handling of the arrangements for the ceremony.

'Blom is the centre of attention, not Anic,' he said.

The Wazir bowed, in pained acknowledgement of this truth.

'What else have you done in my absence?'

The Wazir told him. There was luckily very little that had not already been set in motion or could in any way be thought controversial, but the Akond was also displeased to hear that 'm Baz had been allowed to bring his freak show to the palace, as a likely entertainment for the young Akond.

'You know very well,' he told his Wazir, 'that my tumbling dwarfs could not raise a smile. Why should he be amused at bearded women and albinos and other sports of nature that our impresario friend hauls around the villages in his stinking wagon? This is an amusement for the ignorant, not for the palace.'

'Exaltedness, you are always right,' said Ininin. 'But will you not see it for yourself, since it is already here? It is in the courtyard where they are setting up the stage, and our French guests have expressed an interest in it. It may be that despite your just argument there is some trifling hideous novelty that would amuse the young Akond.'

'We may justly hope that he will be more than amused, in fact, by the Second Gift,' said the Akond. 'But let us look at 'm Baz's collection, if you wish.'

And the Akond went down into the courtyard

with his Wazir, and with Colonel Marzipol and Captain Debussy, who were invited to join them.

'm Baz was confident that his fee would be distinctly augmented by the inclusion of his freaks, and suggested that they be brought before the young Akond in a colourful procession. Although he bowed frequently to the Akond and his guests in token deference, his enthusiasm ran away with him and he did not, in his fussing and chattering, notice the growing coldness of the Akond.

'Here', he said, 'is my Human Skeleton, a man miraculously living without a scrap of flesh on him.'

The Human Skeleton stared at the royal party without interest, and then went on examining his long nails, which grew in scrolls of varying diameters and could, if he compressed them, be just about lightly contained in the palm of the hand.

'Does he not take sustenance?' asked Colonel Marzipol.

'He lives on air, sir,' replied 'm Baz. 'Air and flies.'

'Flies might be enough,' remarked Captain Debussy. 'In sufficient quantities.'

'Here is my Hairy Woman,' said 'm Baz.

She sat patiently on a stool, while he used a painted baton to part the long hairs on her chest and shoulders and to lift up the beard to reveal its fullness.

'Remarkable,' said Colonel Marzipol, bowing to the woman when she smiled at him.

'And here', said 'm Baz, 'is my Mermaid, and my Giant Maggot.'

It was hard to tell whether these creatures were alive or not, and hard enough to see them at all at the bottom of their baskets, though the Maggot seemed to stir amongst its leaves. There was a smell of dust and offal. 'm Baz moved rapidly on through his collection, which contained several amiable singing dwarfs, a stuffed goat with two heads, and a man with a member resembling a solomon tree.

'Not all of this may be entirely suitable to the occasion,' said Colonel Marzipol to the Akond.

'That is evidently true,' said the Akond. 'And I never expected that any of it would be.'

'They are commonplaces of the fairs,' said Captain Debussy. 'The Maggot is a trick, although I do not know how it is done.'

'Exaltedness!' cried 'm Baz. 'Gentlemen! My menagerie is unique, and long in the collecting. It is a humble thing, though it has pleased many. Now I am sure that you will be impressed by my latest acquisition, a wild boy with four legs found in the woods of Wajlat.'

And 'm Baz brought them before 'l Isilik's wicker cage, where the shrouded boy looked out at them from his stench with round eyes of alarm, pain and reproof.

'You will understand, Exaltedness,' said 'm Baz, 'that unlike my Human Skeleton and my Hairy Woman and these others that you have seen, who are proud to display their unique qualities to a discerning and paying public, this boy is truly wild, and must be kept in confinement or else he would escape and attack us all with an uncontrollable ferocity.'

He prodded 'l Isilik with his baton and used its pointed end with swift rough movements to throw back the garment that hid the boy's head and upper body, revealing clearly to the company the extra legs that he possessed, lying inertly across his chest, the feet beneath his chin.

'Hah!' said Debussy, leaning forward with sudden interest. 'A true omphalosite, I do believe.'

He reached his hand into the cage to hold one of the ankles of these extra legs, that were now dressed in pantaloons and red silk slippers, turning 'l Isilik's intimate shame, the whole cause of his ever having been rejected and abandoned, the naked presence of otherness that had throughout his short life challenged and defined his sense of self, into a sort of carnival accoutrement, like a parti-coloured homunculus taking a ridiculous plunge into his stomach. And here was the Captain looking as if he was trying to pull it out.

'Hard to tell whether the legs can move of their own accord,' said Debussy, as 'l Isilik drew back from him to the rear of his cage, moaning. 'I should very much like to examine him further.'

But the Akond, who had grown pale with terror, cried out, 'Enough! I do not want to see this thing. Close up the wagon, and take it away! It is an insult and a conspiracy!'

He left the courtyard, his robes billowing behind him, his mind in torment.

The Wazir, who knew as well as his master what was at issue, forced 'm Baz to his knees and put his sword to the fat man's throat.

'What are you trying here, you rascal?' he asked angrily. But 'm Baz was shaking his head in bewilderment, his palms raised in surrender.

'Ah,' said the Hairy Woman tenderly. 'Do not treat our protector so. He is an honourable man, and pays us well for the exhibition of our rare qualities.'

'Not all of us,' said one of the singing dwarfs. 'But you yourself have much to exhibit to him in private, I dare say. And he does not treat the wild boy well.'

'The wild boy is ungrateful for our company,' said the Hairy Woman, pinching the dwarf for his insult.

The wild boy was moaning. He had come to feel that his identity as 'l Isilik, adopted son of 'l Saqi, the respected engineer of Taflat, was no more than an interval of strange dreaming in his hounded life. Even his sense of the civilities of language and its powers was slipping away from him. He huddled in misery at the back of his cage, trying to remember something that might make him feel that the world had not turned on its head again.

'm Baz protested his entire ignorance of the Akond's displeasure, leaving the Wazir uncertain whether to strike off his head or simply order him to remove his cartload of curiosities.

But Captain Debussy came to him, clinking French gold.

'Put up your sword, I pray you, my good man,' he said. 'I feel sure that our friend the Elephant can have intended no insult to the Akond, and whatever the cause of His Exaltedness's displeasure, it cannot surely but evaporate if the Four-Legged Boy is removed. I should like him taken secretly to my apartment and no one need ever see him again. If you can accomplish this, there is a purse for you, and for 'm Baz, in compensation for his young freak.'

Ininin was uneasy at the proposal (haltingly translated for him by Marzipol), for he was terrified of offending the Akond; while 'm Baz protested at the insufficiency of the offered *louis* as payment for 'l Isilik. To him, Captain Debussy said, 'You are lucky, sir, that the Wazir's sword is now sheathed. You have given offence, and would be wise to rid yourself of the occasion of it and take my generous purse.'

Once 'm Baz, snivelling unconvincingly into his sleeve, had consented to Debussy's proposal, Ininin, too, took his gold.

'The cage must be covered,' he said, 'and taken to the kitchens of the quarters of the palace guard, which are but eighty or so yards from this point, and your own men can then handle it. I shall have nothing to do with it, and if you are discovered shall deny all knowledge of it. And this is on condition, as you have promised, that the boy will never be seen again. I dare not ask what it is that you propose to do to him.'

Colonel Marzipol, again translating, laughed.

'I think I can guess,' he said. 'Captain Debussy is a surgeon of great boldness and resource, compelled on the battlefield to some pretty complicated, if rough-and-ready, procedures. I am sure that he is as curious as I am to know what these extra legs are attached to, perhaps to relieve the boy of them if he can.'

'To relieve him of them?' inquired the Wazir, weakly. He was aware from conversations at court of the illimitable intellectual curiosity and technical skills of the French savants, but for the moment could not apply such a rational project to his conception of 'l Isilik, who was a secret calamity of the royal house that he had served all his life, perhaps a sign of the gods' mysterious displeasure, and a haunting symbol of some disaster to come. 'Is that possible?'

'Captain Debussy has a cool nerve and a steady hand,' said Colonel Marzipol cheerily. 'When Colonel Cagoule's chin was shot away in Holland, he sewed the skin of his neck to his upper lip on the same afternoon. Two weeks later Cagoule was back in Paris receiving all his sustenance through a tube, in good spirits and able faintly to articulate.'

'Remarkable,' said the Wazir.

As the cage was taken away disguised as a basket

of vegetables, some sort of faint articulation might have been heard from it by anyone who had paid it attention. It was the voice of 'l Isilik, half-succeeding at last in cheering himself up:

> 'One, two, three, four, five:
> Where will the swimmer dive?
> Six, seven, eight, nine, ten:
> Into the fire and back again.'

20

THAT evening, the Akond called for the palace scribe and by the light of an oil lamp composed an official letter in which the revelation of the unaccountably and hideously surviving 'l Isilik was, though not of course far from his mind, naturally no part of his theme. The letter cleared a certain part of his mind of a significant lumber of thoughts that had occupied it, but in itself, when it was completed, gave him little satisfaction, for his mind was then left occupied by the image of his first-born son, in a wicker cage:

'To his Imperial Majesty, Napoleon Bonaparte, all greetings and respectful salutations from His Exaltedness, Bedr 'l Ashal Blemim in-Blemim, Akond of Taflat, &c., &c.

'My liberty in writing to you is taken without the knowledge of our long-time guests and friends, the military detachment of your countrymen who have adventured here to Taflat, although their presence here is at least the occasion of my writing, and not least its subject.

'I fear that this military party may be in trouble for notable disobedience to orders, and for that reason I shall refer to them all indiscriminately by allusion to their leading officer, Colonel M——. The recent Peace of Amiens may not have been an occasion for according amnesty to deserters, though it has (as Colonel M—— originally proposed to me, with great prescience) been the occasion for your own *recoiling* in order to be *sauté'd,* as I think the French tongue has it, for now you are no longer merely your country's greatest General and Consul for life, but its Emperor. In that role, you stand outside the ordinary mechanics of military discipline and embody the many royal prerogatives of healing, judging, pardoning, and indeed of creating the laws themselves.

'I know well the personal burden of such powers. How may we discriminate between a cowardly opportunism and a largeness of venturing spirit? Between self-interest and the deeper patriotism that belongs to the imagination? From my now considerable knowledge of Colonel M——, I can vouch for abundant qualities of the latter virtues. In his case, should it ever come to your notice (which I trust it may), there would be the question not of rebuke for ignoring orders but of reward for extending the interests of France and of her Empire.

'Your evident vision of an Empire of Europe to balance the Empire of the Ottomans is a distraction to the Porte that we, lying adjacent to Turkish influence, would deeply welcome. Equally, subjugation of the British and their interests in India would please us. I would not claim that we are leant upon from either side, or quarrelled over as desert hyenas argue a bone, for we here at Taflat have long preserved a vigorous independence in our geographical position and in our complex secrets of agriculture and trade, having given up warfare altogether. It is a mysterious truth that a country that has no army tends to provoke no invasions, and there is little strategic mastery to be gained here within the dissolving margins of opposed powers. With our liberal port of Taflat your citizens freely trade, and I am told that there are many commodities leaving our docks which would be otherwise unavailable to you in time of war. Should you wish to consolidate these trading interests with a Treaty, I can assure you of considerate and friendly terms, guaranteed by the presence here of Colonel M——, who is qualified in every natural characteristic, save for Letters of

Appointment, to act as your Ambassador.

'When you were turned back in your beneficent eastwards advance by Sir Sidney Smith, you no doubt reflected that since it was not from weariness, like Alexander at the Indus, the disappointment would remain a frustration to plague you with regrets for ever. I have no doubt (if you will forgive the assertion) that this can no longer be the case, for the reversal will on the contrary have impelled your resolve to consolidate a union of the kingdoms and principalities of your own continent by both military and dynastic means, and therefore to create (as it were) a United States of Europe. The world will applaud such a civilising idea, for in the future, throughout such an empire, the usual wars of covetous princes will surely be unknown.

'It is covetousness, ambition and jealousy in both the public and private spheres of life which is the death of honour, since all loyalties (between prince and subject, brother and brother, husband and wife, &c.) are destroyed by these passions. Honour should be recognised in whatever class of life it may be found, and its adherents admitted into a formal company of virtuous behaviour. Such a Legion would reflect upon the essential virtue of a nation as a whole, the civil as much as the military, and I recommend it for your consideration.

'Not even the personal salvation of the individual should take precedence over honour and virtue. There is a class of Jain monks called the Digambara (the "sky-clad") who pursue a life of utter self-abnegation and simplicity. But to turn your back on the world in stasis and nakedness is not necessarily, as I am sure you will agree, to lead a virtuous life, which cannot be virtuous unless exposed to ordinary temptations.

'An Emperor may not himself choose the celibate life, since he must secure the succession, and this is an excellent thing, because thereby he is exposed to the ordinary assaults upon emotional integrity which the family life imposes. You can see that in this matter I have been instructed by the reasoning of my guests, your compatriots, for whom the mind is the Emperor itself of the rebel human senses and their super-stitions. I trust that your own succession will soon be put on a proper footing of filial inheritance, for it cannot be right that your heir-designate remain for long your brother Joseph. You will forgive my offering you this advice, I trust, for I know very well the unreliability of brothers, who are never satisfied with their accorded station in life but will always be after more, or indeed anything which is nominally forbidden them. I could wish my own brother Anic, a simple and straightforward man in many respects, to have more of the Digambara in his constitution, for I fear his jealousy of me and of what is mine.

'I myself have an heir, who tomorrow is to be presented with his bride. This is a significant stage of our process of inheritance, for he will enter upon his seven years of adult pleasure, and in seven years' time will succeed to the kingdom and beget his own heir. I write to you on the eve of this event in a spirit of friendly greeting and exhortation, with this warning about brothers. However fond we may be of them, however trusting in the ties of blood and common parentage, they may deceive us. For myself, I plan to exile my brother Anic to our spice plantations in the north in the place of my father, the former Akond, who is unhappy there. And instead of myself inheriting their administration in seven years' time when I in turn cease to be Akond, I shall send out Anic's eldest son to join him, and embrace my retirement in the happier company of my father.

'Our lives are so circumscribed by these traditions, designed to make best use of the talents and energy of the young, that the old are often rendered useless and anxious. Since the young all inevitably become old at some time or other, it would be better either not to please them by such an early bestowing of power and responsibility, or at least to make life better in its aftermath.

'But this is a solution to a particular problem of ours, and of little interest to you. It has exemplary value only, not least because it is the product of reason and not of unthinking tradition. I do not intend a revolution. It is the example of Colonel M— and his compatriots that encourages me to fight all non-thinking wherever I find it. Irrational fears, terrible accidents, conspiracies, destructive egotism, craven superstitions, these plague the civilised life just as dropsies and fevers do.

'Thus I leave you in the spirit of your own savants and philosophes, unworthy of their achievements, but ambitious to follow the instructive workings of their minds.

'Emperor, in brotherhood I address you! For the brotherhood of the spirit and of the public life is of a power to rival the brotherhood of the blood!'

21

HAD Dibl been bribed, thought the Akond? For some reason, and very likely an illicit one, he had been unable to wrest the headless goat from Anic although he threw himself at the Akond's brother as they ritually galloped against each other, and appeared to throw himself hard. His hands could get no purchase on the animal, however, and several times he was himself unseated. The other players took courage from this reversal and many of the young courtiers similarly prevailed against the players from Ormund. Anic, in turn, had much greater success against Dibl, and in one tourney seized the goat with one arm, hooking it beneath his elbow.

Turning to the other members of the party who were watching from the shade of their tent to share his surprise at this outcome, in-Blemim noticed immediately the confusion in the darting eyes of Juliba.

And what, then, is this, he thought? What has happened during my absence? Is this evidence of a betrayal that I have long feared?

Anic was laughing before him, drenched in sweat like the shrine of a god in the monsoon, his teeth gleaming, his chest deeply heaving still with the exertion. The goat was flung on the ground between them.

'A gift for Blom!' he panted. 'A gift for the noble young Akond!'

Blom looked away in embarrassment, his heavy eyelids lowered disdainfully, and for once in-Blemim was too preoccupied with his own thoughts to be ashamed of him. Anic's eyes looked merrily at each of the royal party in turn, as a great roar of approval went up round the field, and his eyes were seen to linger longest on Juliba.

And Juliba was transfixed. In the privacy of her veil, she blushed.

Two palace slaves hoisted Anic on their shoulders and paraded him round the field, but before the circuit was half-completed the Akond motioned impatiently to his Wazir, and the royal party were hastily conducted to their litters and returned to the palace.

Colonel Marzipol, who had watched all this with an observant eye, took the first opportunity to discuss it with Captain Orqueban.

'Is this not further evidence that behind the calm exterior of this court there is much intrigue and passion?' he asked.

'Decidedly,' said Orqueban. 'There are all the secrets here that you might suspect of a system that attempts to impose a rational control of our animal nature.'

'Meaning?'

'I mean that our Akond leads a celibate life,' replied Orqueban. 'Having produced his heir, he has no function but to rule his little kingdom. It is enough to make any red-blooded man wither into a premature dotage.'

'And that leaves the queen Juliba . . .?'

'Precisely,' said Orqueban. 'She is open to every temptation, and if she should devote herself to her son instead, then she would be equally distracted by the elaborate preparations for his period of licensed indulgence in the pleasures of the flesh. What mother can bear to face her son's maturity?'

'Which is why it would appear that the preparations are in the hands not of the mother but the grandmother,' said Marzipol. 'It is she who instructs the young Akond's bride in all the rituals of the bedchamber. Can you imagine the strange school of lust being conducted in the closed apartments of the palace?' Marzipol's bright eyes performed a merry dance.

'I wonder that the Akond himself does not defy custom, and pursue some secret assignation,' said Orqueban.

'Perhaps he does,' replied Marzipol. 'How would we know?'

'I think his temperament is cold, and his veins sluggish,' said Orqueban. 'Look at the son he produced: a milksop.'

'Blom is a clever boy,' retorted Marzipol. 'And he has feelings. But the active life is not for him.'

'Well, he is to be wed tonight, God help him.'

'Indeed,' said Marzipol. 'And do you not find it marvellously strange that our friend Debussy, begging to be excused from the entertainment, is proposing, on the very night that the young Akond is to be made one flesh with his bride, to sever the omphalosite into two persons?'

'From what you have told me, I do not believe it can be done. Suppose there are only one and a half persons?'

'I agree,' said Marzipol. 'That is an extremely uncomfortable calculation. After all, they say that

God is indivisible because the Trinity may not be halved, and you and I in our childhood could never have shared three marbles. How much less could one-and-a-half be easily divided? Let us go to Debussy and find out just what he intends. From the Akond's reaction to the boy, I sense that there is another secret here, for I would guess that he is not a stranger to the deformity.'

'l Isilik was lodged in a small attic room in the quarters of the palace guard, freed from his cage, but watched by the French orderlies. Captain Debussy had obtained some leather harness which he had caused to be attached to a sort of carved tallboy inlaid with ivory which had been brought in from another room.

'You have not wasted time,' said Colonel Marzipol, when he saw it. The boy was crouched in a corner of the room, terrified. The orderlies were playing faro.

'I see no profit in delay,' replied Captain Debussy. 'But this arrangement will not do. It is too high for me to perform the operation, and the legs are too short, so that even if I have them sawn off it will not make enough difference.'

'And a table?' suggested Marzipol.

'Have you yet seen anything like a table in this country, Colonel?' said Debussy. 'We eat here off the carpets, as at a Trianon pique-nique. I have folded my legs so many times into an unaccustomed squat, that I walk with a hobble like an old woman gathering firewood.'

Orqueban approached 'l Isilik in his corner with a wary diplomatic grin, and 'l Isilik looked back at him with narrowed eyes, as at the latest and least considerable of a carnival of demons.

'Doesn't this boy remind you of someone?' he remarked to the other two over his shoulder.

'From my nightmares,' said Debussy, 'or some Flemish Inferno.'

'No, I mean his features.'

Marzipol joined Orqueban in his scrutiny, dropping to his haunches to stare into the boy's face.

'You are right,' he said. 'I didn't notice it before, but he looks just like the young Akond. Though more handsome.'

'Akond,' said the boy loudly in assent. 'Akond.'

They did not know what to make of this repetition, save as an unthinking repetition of a word just said. But 'l Isilik had intended it as the expression of something that he was in the process of perceiving, the connection between the ruler of his country and himself. For what 'm Ezla may have said to 'm Fega, and what he may have said to 'm Baz, in the presence of his victim, presumed an idiot, could easily have been put together to make a kind of conclusion: that the Akond would be significantly interested in him, that there were dangers in the secret, that his destiny was finally to be brought to the palace by whatever means, and for whatever purpose.

And so, here he was.

And together, the French soldiers examined him. They divested his rudimentary twin of the silk pantaloons and slippers which 'm Baz had provided, to give him the agreeable comical air of a clownish performance. Indeed, Captain Orqueban said that it reminded him of a village entertainment of his youth, where a man appearing to ride upon the back of another who was running at incredible speed on his hands, was in truth himself doing the running, dressed within the effigy of another whose front protruded from his waist with false legs hanging down in little stirrups on either side, and with his own feet in shoes made to look like hands.

'It is strange', said Colonel Marzipol, 'that nature herself will occasionally imitate these tricks which acrobats play, who like to balance on each other's shoulders or knees, and are so adept that they seem to grow there, and move about as one, perfectly at their ease.'

'But look,' said Captain Debussy. 'In this case it is as though one so balancing has slipped and plunged into his belly. The feet and toes are perfectly formed, and see, when I stroke the sole of the left foot there is a reflex action, and the toes extend towards the chin! There is much less animation of this kind in the right foot, and nothing that you might credibly call a joint at the knee. The groin is attached just below the rib-cage, and the deformed and rudimentary trunk appears as a swelling across the epigastrium. The boy's navel appeared at first to be completely hidden, which, as you will realise, made me wonder how he could have been born. But look, here it is behind this protuberance which is like a shoulder!'

'Extraordinary!' exclaimed Marzipol.

'You may imagine a buried head,' continued Debussy, 'speaking through the boy's fundament, or whose drowned eyes act as the generators of the seed of venery, imaging the coined beauty of desire in their perpetual darkness.'

'You are a surgeon, sir,' said the Colonel, 'and

must not let your fancy run away with you. There can be no space in the poor boy's body for a head, and I sincerely hope that you do not propose to go looking for one.'

Debussy's pasty face broke momentarily into a fixed false smile.

'Oh yes,' he replied, 'I rather think I do.'

And he gestured decisively at the thin array of his instruments set out upon a napkin, polished as if for military inspection: the curved silver knives with chased handles, the needles, the forceps, the cauterising tubes, the awls with their shining brass bits, the straps.

22

WHEN the stomach of the buffalo was cut open, the fat glistened in glutinous veils down the skin of the beast and from its entrails spilled raisins, dates, almonds, tamarinds and little trussed corpses of the birds that used in life to perch between the buffalo's horns, relieving it of the insects that made its life a misery. In death, therefore, not misery but culinary glory, if less than glorious for the birds. But at least their bodies did not contain tiny marinaded or crispened samples of the insects they had so usefully devoured, though the palace cook at one point contemplated the notion with some hopeful enthusiasm. Finally, there emerged from this fertile mountain of stuffing a small vigorous shape like an oiled acrobatic baby, who immediately burst into song:

'Westward, O love, where light finishes
          Its long travelling!
     O horizon where light vanishes!
          O unravelling

A Tale

Of our reflections, O coloured arc!
    O independence
Of the ideal in the absence of light!
    O transcendence
Of human form in the encompassing night!
    O promise of love in the perfect dark!'

The women of the court feigned to faint with pleasure, but the old Akond smiled to himself. A pretty epithalamion, he thought, to be warbled by a singing dwarf, naked as a baby. We are generated in darkness, and return to it eagerly in our shame. And does not that sensual darkness betoken its colder brother, which is eternal?

The drummers beat the tightened skins of their instruments to a climax as Blom was served with the sweet private organs of the buffalo in honour of his impending Gift. The dwarf somersaulted away across the carpets, turning through a paper hoop at the door, where, by a consummate trick of the court conjuror, he became on the further side of it not a dwarf at all, but a fair young girl who bowed gracefully to the company and threw blossoms about.

Yet, reflected the old Akond as he ate, life may surprise us still. There may occur unforeseen events which will reverse the dull course of our expectation. Who, for example, could have known that at this moment I would be seated here at my grandson's Gift and not pursuing phantoms of idle pleasure and regret at Samira? This freedom to command the reversion of exile bodes well (he thought), for if we may thus return into our real lives in a moment, without any prior expectation of it, what else may not be achieved? In-Blemim is a philosopher, but he is also the Akond, and the world is at his command. When I lamented the passing of the years, he wisely urged me not to consider the stages towards death but to find some occupation. When I complained that I had already used up one-third of my portion, he rightly pointed out that I had yet twice as much left. When this comforting thought was no longer true, and I had only one-third left, he advised me to live for each moment of life as it came to me. How can this be done, when we also seek the transcendence just celebrated by that greasy dwarf? The words of the poet are most apposite:

'Time after time after time
The thought of everything
Defeats us, every time.

A Tale

Taking it thing by thing
By thing, taking our time,
That might be the thing.

But now it seems that time
Itself is everything,
And there is never time

To deal with anything
Decisively, for time
Too has become a thing.

We always feel there's time
To see some faultless thing
Standing there outside time.

We can only take one thing,
Singly, at a time:
Thought is good for nothing.'

The thing, in any case, thought uz-Blemim, whatever it may be is outside us as well, and all we are is a
continuum of impressions. To be well is enough. To
be completely well an unlooked-for joy. To notice a
thing, to isolate it within one's consciousness, is
immediately to be full of apprehension. Our relationship with the thing is unresolved. Even to name it

gives it an undue significance within the general frame of things.

Not to think at all, perhaps. Except that there is still a comfort in the paradox that arriving at the expected moment may never be strictly possible, in that to conceive of the moment as in some way forever receding before us, for example by living only half-way towards it, however far off it yet may be, and then reassessing the distance, living only half-way towards that new point, and so on, puts it always beyond experience. But these points must be marked, like the bell of a feast or the promise of an hour on a dial: how possible would that be?

The old Akond decided to tell no one about these plans, not even his son, who seemed preoccupied with troubles of his own. He suspected that some error in his reasoning might be readily pointed out to him, for after all it could not be thought credible that a man might be certain, however old he might become, that he always had more than half the remaining portion of his life left to live. There was a trick in it, certainly, but he did not want it pointed out to him, not just at the moment, when sherbets were being brought, and steaming napkins, and the drummers of the feast were replaced by lutes and singers.

A Tale

We have feasted, thought the old Akond, and though we feel that we shall never wish to feast again, we know in certainty that we shall do so.

As was invariably the custom, the diners now removed to the balconies of the courtyard, where the stage was ready for the masque to celebrate the presentation of Ahraz to the young Akond. The royal party were garlanded with flowers, and their cushions sprinkled with the rarest of perfumes. The singers and lute-players stood nearby, warbling in muted tones of the delights of connubial love.

Blom was carried on a palanquin to his own dais of audience. He supposed that his parents, and the court in general, were interested enough in the coming spectacle not to be exclusively concerned with watching him, but he was nervous none the less. There they all were, ranged above him: his mother, his grandmother, his great-grandmother, the ladies of the private apartments, the mothers of Anic's children; the Wazir, the Chamberlain, the counsellors, the officials and guests, the Turkish Resident, the chief merchants, the French officers; and his father and grandfather. He supposed that among the merchants was the father of his princess, come to see her dance.

He did not know that on that very morning 'l Cara had taken poison in despair.

The stage gave the illusion of being empty. The musicians drew down from above a vast red cloth which hung in front of the emptiness. Then they unfolded a length of green silk and let it billow between them on the platform to represent the waters of the nourishing river that rose at Sarapa and passed its blessings across the country as it made its way to the sea. An explosion of sulphurous fire was seen momentarily behind the red cloth which the musicians then drew away to reveal what had not seemed to be there before: an enormous shape constructed of cane and painted silk. It was rounded and full at one end with an outlet like a narrowing cave, and pointed at the other. The audience gasped at its sudden appearance, and the smoke from the firework drifted across the courtyard.

Now the musicians settled themselves in a corner of the stage and began the continuous drumming that was to accompany the dance. The shape, having mysteriously descended in a flash of light, was now only dimly defined, but all eyes were upon it.

It seemed to some onlookers like a flower, to others a fruit. Some thought it perhaps a fountain, and those with literal minds believed it to be a cave. Blom considered it to be a representation of his shell, and so did his grandfather who had given it to him. Those who saw the bell of a flower, heard it buzz with music like a trapped bee; for those who saw a fruit, it seemed heavy with life; as a fountain, it looked ready to burst forth; if it were a cave, it must contain treasure; if it were a shell, a god must sound within it. But perhaps it was all of these things, as well as being a giant representation of the secret parts of generation of the promised princess, from which she herself would yet emerge in a second birth of love.

Only uz-Blemim, remembering the frenzy of the women who had left Samira to become votaries of the mountain god, was disturbed to see the shell as the locus of the Gift, for what Akond, however hot-blooded, wishes to see his bride in a frenzy?

Suddenly, in a fine stroke of stagecraft for which 'm Baz had required twenty oil lamps to be instantaneously lit, the shell was illuminated softly from within and the shadow of Ahraz was cast motionless upon the silk. The drumming paused for a heartbeat only, then started up in earnest, as Ahraz lowered her raised hands and came forward, a moth from a persimmon, a bee from an orchid, the surge of water from a fountain, a ruby from a mine, a whisper of infinite power from the mouth of a shell, and began to dance for her young Akond.

Was it indeed a dance of frenzy? Or was it a dance of love's greeting? To the three Akonds, uz-Blemim, in-Blemim and Blom, it spoke a different language according to the nature of their troubled minds. To the older Akonds it was a reminder of the inviting charm of beauty which they had lost or were in the process of losing; to the youngest Akond it was a revealing manifestation of the desire which he knew that life required of him. To the oldest Akond it was the dance of youth which he could no longer possess; to the younger Akonds it was also a moral story which had the power to change the course of their lives.

Ahraz danced in a narrative style brought from beyond the Indus, where each episode of the story was conveyed by gestures of hand and wrist, the fingers encircling the face to emphasise a fleeting emotion and the arms describing arcs to indicate completed actions. Her whole body, from eyebrow to little toe, was active and each part independently alert. The moods of the players in her danced story passed momentarily across her smiling face, bringing its fixed and staring beauty briefly to life as timidity, longing, enticement, fear, rage. And at the conclusion of each episode, like the refrain of a poem, she took a series of formal backward steps, toe to heel, while glancing exaggeratedly first to the left and then to the right, her dark pupils and kohl-lined eyes moving as if by some internal clockwork, accompanied by little jerks of the neck moving in the opposite direction.

Blom stared into her staring face, transfixed. His soul felt prostrated, as before the image of a goddess brought alive by the conjuror's art. The beautiful smile was not quite static: the emotions flickered across her mouth and eyes as shadows cast by the fortunes and fates of the characters she danced. Her body was a moving stage for these characters and not merely the seductive body of a girl. Blom was therefore attracted and distanced at the same time, his growing desire for Ahraz tempered by his attention to the story.

Her arms rose and made the circle which described the throne of the unjust Caliph Razaman. Her knees bent into something like a squat, and she frowned to show him delivering judgements from it. The beggar boy entered: supplication. The boy spoke of his suffering mother: love, tears, hunger, hard labour, all occupying for their few triumphant seconds the impassive but mobile face of the lovely Ahraz.

Drum and pipes described the boy's hopes. Ahraz's feet retreated, toe to heel, to the rear of the stage and back again.

Her left hand traced the Caliph's beard on the burnished oval of her own cheek while her right arm was crooked and uplifted in anger. Was the mother already a slave of the Caliph's? Now the boy will be, too. Darting glances of desperation, left and right. There is no escape from the terrible judgement of the Caliph, who is in no mood to be defied.

Backwards and forwards she retreated and advanced, toe to heel. It was the story of the boy Medona, host to the angel who defeated the unjust Caliph Razaman, as everyone in the audience except the French visitors had recognised.

Colonel Marzipol had thought of whispering to the Akond and asking him for an explanation. Was this to be a tragedy or a comedy? Or was it like a ballet at the Opéra, something about nothing very much at all? But he desisted, for he saw the Akond's face darken, as if something in the performance were displeasing to him.

A Tale

The Akond, for his part, was suddenly abashed to see this representation of a ruler without charity. Had he authorised the subject of the dance? Surely not. He had wanted a dance about a ruler who was an evident hero. He had naturally suggested the subject of Napoleon, but Ininin had told him that there was no tradition of dancing such a story and that therefore uz-Mabmabla could not possibly teach it to Ahraz. Besides, Napoleon's story, such as it was, was still unfinished. How, then, could a dance about him be given an ending?

As Ahraz danced on, the shameful story unfolded of Razaman's tyranny over the mother of Medona, and of Medona's revenge. Medona's starved body, bowed by the chains of Razaman's deepest dungeon, became the host to an angel spirit which descended in the night and occupied the space inside his skin entirely, giving him the strength to break his chains and escape from the dungeon.

When Ahraz danced the angel entering the boy Medona, she seemed to grow six inches in stature, and a wild smile flitted across her face, almost too quickly to be seen. The drums increased their pace.

Backwards and forwards she retreated and advanced, toe to heel. There was much to be revealed still in her story: how Razaman had usurped his brother's throne and exiled him to the land of the midget leopards who, if he remained still in one place for more than ten minutes, would eat him alive; how Medona acquired supernatural powers and fought against a hundred valiant soldiers of the Caliph's guard, who pursued him to the highest pinnacle of the palace; how the Caliph came to him there, and as they fought shoulder to shoulder, knee to knee, they rose higher into the air, and knew that the first to look down would fall.

Backwards and forwards, toe to heel. The frown on Ahraz's face cast barely a shadow on her impassive beauty. The fighting was in the drums, and in the flick of her wrists and reversals of her pointing fingers. Her feet were bare and painted red, with thick ropes of bells on the ankles and chains looped from the ankles over the arches of her feet. She stamped with her heels, and the stage thundered. She stamped, and again bent her knees into the position of masculine authority that was like a crouch before a pounce.

Blom was entranced and appalled. Was this fierce remote creature truly to be brought to his bed? Who could instruct him in the ceremonies that their encounter that night would be bound to require? She was as young as he was, he had been told. But she seemed like an ageless spirit, an angel herself, a perfect embodiment of the impartial justice required by her story, whereby the rightful Caliph would be restored, the enslaved mother of Medona released and even the hordes of miniature leopards defeated and put to some useful domestic purpose.

When it was all explained later to Colonel Marzipol, and he was told how Razaman was the first to look down and the first to fall because he was under the illusion that a flying serpent was gnawing at his foot, and how Razaman was himself restored to life and forgiven, he twirled his moustaches upwards and smiled.

'It has, peculiarly enough, all the elements of a Christian story,' he mused to himself. 'And all performed to perfection by that delicious little savage. She is wasted on the young Akond, poor fellow. He will surely treat her like the merest gambit at chess, and forgo whatever she has been taught to offer him as though it were a trap. It is partly my fault, I think, because I failed to explain the genius of Philidor, but I also believe it to be in his nature. If in seven years' time he makes me his Wazir, I could show her a trick or two that he will have missed.'

After the entertainments of the day, it was now time for the pleasures of the night, and the incense-bowls were lit all along the terraces.

23

WHEN later Anic burst into Juliba's chamber, grinning with foolish assurance, he had naturally not expected to find his brother hidden within the hangings of the bed.

'Well?' said the Akond, holding out his sabre at arm's length, its unwavering point not a foot from Anic's beard. 'Well?'

'Brother, you have me,' said Anic, the smile on his face replaced by pallor, his arms helplessly loose at his side, the palms forward.

'And you, brother, have nothing,' replied the Akond.

'It is the lottery of birth, brother,' said Anic. 'It would have been better had I not been born, for I have no power and no inheritance.'

'It is so,' said in-Blemim.

'And perhaps in the case of Blom you have been wise in your abstention,' continued Anic, 'for should he have had a younger brother, that brother would surely have been pitied, as I am pitied and laughed at in the palace, for his uselessness.'

The Akond was stung in his heart by this argument, not so much by pity for his brother, as by the thought of Blom who was in truth himself still a younger brother after all, and therefore perhaps like Anic by nature unsuited to a throne. He lowered the sabre, and took his brother by the arm.

'Is it not the case', said, 'that we seek the happiness appropriate to our nature? You are unhappy here because you are not the Akond, and you desire to lie with Juliba because you are not the Akond. I can think of no other reason for this. But I do not think that you would be happy to be the Akond. You are happy in the thoughtless life of the body and its exploits, and you would prefer to be racing your yacht about the harbour at Taflat or finding the means to pleasure four Chinese concubines at one time, to the rule of a kingdom or the dispensing of justice.'

'How can I agree,' replied Anic, 'having had no chance to rule? How do I know? How do you know?'

'Well, we shall see,' said in-Blemim. And he informed his brother of his intention to send him to the administration of the spice fields in the place of their father.

Anic looked dismayed.

'What will I do there? How will this make me happy?'

'It isn't intended to make you happy, but it is logical. You will have the opportunity to do what our father wished to do but could not bring himself to the point of doing, which is to build a palace of pleasure. The wish was not in his nature, just as it is not in your real nature to wish to be me. We must all find the means to be ourselves.'

In-Blemim dismissed his brother, and brought Juliba out of her hiding.

'You often say that I do not care for you,' he said, 'but that is not true. You came to me because I am the Akond, and I came to you because you were my Gift, as Ahraz is Blom's Gift. You have no existence without me, and now I know that despite being the Akond I have no existence without you. This is our fate and nature, like the course of the river and the water that flows within it.'

Juliba looked up from her shame, and her glance rekindled in the Akond's eyes the fire of her own dancing. He embraced her, and continued: 'My father has defied tradition in returning from Samira, and I shall defy tradition by never going there. We shall remain here with you and uz-Mabmabla, even though in our age we shall be but shadows of men.'

Juliba privately thought that perhaps all men were but shadows, for the light fell on them and they cast their image about with little effort and no pain, but she said nothing, hardly knowing whether she liked in-Blemim's renewed vows more than she regretted Anic's exile. For Blom's sake at least she was readier for the former.

And what, in this mood of change and reconciliation, should the Akond now do for Blom's sake?

In dealing with his brother, he had been sharply seized with the idea that our roles in life may be misappropriated by individuals or by custom, and sometimes by both. If our happiness consists in being ourselves, how may we know what exactly our selves are, when circumstances may define them falsely for us, or when we fret under such definitions, not knowing if they may be true or not?

He called for the Wazir.

'Where is the boy?' he demanded.

'Exaltedness, which boy do you mean?' responded Ininin, looking about him for some clue to this interest of the Akond's.

'The boy in the basket, the wild boy, the boy with

the legs, the baby that was mine that you failed to get rid of . . . the young Akond!' shouted in-Blemim with mounting fury. 'I do not know why I do not have your head for this incompetence. You defy me at every turn!'

'Exaltedness, you told me to send him away,' said Ininin, bowing his head. Why had his master now called him 'the young Akond'?

'I told you to take him away fifteen years ago,' said the Akond. 'How is it that he comes back, now of all times?'

The Wazir saw his chance.

'Now, Exaltedness? It must be the will of the gods.'

'Do not speak to me of gods,' said the Akond, 'for I do not believe that you know yourself which ones you profess to believe in.'

'It must be fated, Exaltedness,' said Ininin.

He was still uncertain of his master's intentions in the matter, and looked at him expectantly for some clue.

'I told you to be rid of him, and not for the first time, but you did not obey me,' said the Akond. 'And the disobedience was not for the first time, either. I know you did not obey me, for the dwarf that came out of the buffalo was a singing dwarf. It was not one of the palace dwarfs, who have all had their tongues removed for insolence, so it must have been one of the dwarfs from 'm Baz's wagon of curiosities. The wagon must still be here. And therefore the boy must still be here.'

The clue was slow in coming. The Wazir cleared his throat.

'Exaltedness, what is your wish in this matter?' he asked.

'I wish you to speak clearly,' said the Akond, 'unless you also want to lose your tongue.'

The Wazir was forced to confess that Captain Debussy had taken the boy away with a scientific eagerness to remove the superfluous legs and discover what they might be attached to. The Akond was relieved to hear that the boy was at hand, but appalled at what he might suffer at the hands of a battlefield surgeon.

'The man will kill him!' he exclaimed. 'Does he think that it is like extracting a tooth?'

When they at last reached the attic room in the military block, the guards melting before them one by one in deference, the lamps flickering on the staircases as though to light a hunt at night for something that haunts a public building in search of a private resting-place, they found only Captain Debussy in his shirt, with one of his orderlies. A little brazier glowed, on which his instruments were heating in a grid.

Debussy seemed unembarrassed, and slightly drunk.

'The boy has the strength of a pack of wolves,' he said. 'One mouthful of this and he was out of the window like a ball from a musket.'

He described a vague circle at them with the bottle in his hand. It was *aqua dente*, a rough liquor made of dates, intended for the patient, to make the surgery conceivable, and now clearly being consumed instead by the surgeon.

'He bit one of my orderlies' fingers to the bone,' he said cheerfully. 'When he brings him back I shall have to stitch it up first, damn it. Do these muddling roofs lead anywhere in particular?'

The Akond was torn between anger, his confusion about his intentions with regard to 'l Isilik, and a residual politeness to his guest.

'The boy is not what you think he is,' he said, 'and I am afraid that I must forbid you to perform any kind of operation on him. If you find him, you will bring him to me.'

But neither the Akond nor the Captain understood one another, since it was only Colonel Marzipol who had made any attempt to learn the language. All the Captain knew was that the Akond did not appear to be able to make up his mind: first he was offended by the boy and wanted to be rid of him, and now he was angry and wanted to find him.

Captain Debussy goggled at the Akond, and took another swig of *aqua dente*. The Akond swept his instruments to the floor, and stormed out of the room, convinced that the evening's dancing had exposed him as being as unjust and misled as the wicked Caliph Razaman.

24

WITHIN the hangings of Blom's bed there was torment of a different kind.

The eunuchs had brought the Gift on velvet cushions from the women's apartments in an open chair of gilded cane, and Blom had received them in his room, standing formally at the front of the carpeted platform where his bed stood, his hands clasped together for no other reason than that he could think of nowhere else to put them without looking as though he were his father reviewing the palace guard. The eunuchs had lowered the chair and handed the Gift from it as gently as gardeners transplanting a flower. There was wine, and fruits and sweetmeats laid out on silver dishes, and a gentle light stirring in the corners of the room. And then the eunuchs, together with the remaining servants, had retreated respectfully.

What had Blom been meant to do?

He was most forcibly reminded of the occasion of his First Gift, when he had been dressed up to be introduced to his little horse. The horse had sedately performed for him, trotting round in a circle with mincing steps, tossing its plaited mane like a conjuror's coloured streamers. It hadn't, it seemed to him, ever offered itself as a serious riding experience. It had acted the part of a horse already being controlled and ridden, with constrained movements of the legs and the occasional sidewards drift like a ketch in the wind, nodding its head up and down and snorting with apparent satisfaction at its own willingness to have been tamed. How should he have mounted this pert equine automaton? It was a self-sufficient creature, beautiful in its way, but to Blom in his clumsiness quite unapproachable.

It was the same with his bride. As the horse performed, so the girl had danced, and the dance itself was perfect beyond any physical relationship that he could credibly imagine himself initiating with her. The grace of her movements, the suppleness of her body and the discipline of her limbs, had so defined and contained the story she had danced that there was no role left for Blom to play. She herself had become Medona inhabited by the angel, her torso strained erect and flushed by the invading spirit. Transformed, her telling of the defeat of the wicked

Caliph was like a sword which cut to the heart of a revealed truth. Through her, the overthrow of deceit, jealousy and betrayal was for that moment the inevitable end to which all human action stirred itself, Medona victorious, and Razaman humbled.

'Tell me a story,' said Blom.

There was at this quite naturally a moment of alarm, for Ahraz knew the stories of the Thousand Nights and One Night, where King Shahryar out of a despair at the faithlessness of women caused a virgin to be brought nightly to his bed and then had her beheaded. She knew of the Wazir's daughter Shahrazad, who postponed her fate at the hands of the king by telling him stories that he could not bear should be left unfinished.

She stared at Blom with such thoughts in her head, and then she laughed.

And Blom, who knew the stories, too, laughed with her.

'No,' she said. 'That sounds dangerous.'

The ice between them was broken, and Ahraz climbed up with him on to the bed. She untied his robe and let it fall about him, and she unbuttoned his tunic. Her hand splayed on his chest told him how fast his heart was beating.

We can do anything you like,' she said, her mind running frantically over the endless clauses, sub-clauses, provisos and footnotes of her instructions. She had never understood how it was possible to codify, categorise and predict all the whims of pleasure. Nor quite how much of it she was supposed to initiate herself.

Blom beamed at her politely.

They were seated on the bed with their knees folded, lotus-fashion. If anyone had chanced to see them he would have instinctively looked for a chess-board between them, and perhaps for a pattern of pieces that indicated a momentary crisis in the conflict, the possibility of risky sacrifice or too early a draw. As it was, each smiled in expectation across the little void between them. And for something to do, Ahraz reached out her other hand and drew close the curtains of the bed.

The torment was of a kind that Blom thought he might be glad to revisit in order to see how it might lead in other directions than the one it appeared swiftly to take. This invasion of the space about him that he imagined he owned because it defined the shape of his body seemed most like teasing or bully-ing, but because it was accompanied by surprising vistas of another body clearly intending him no harm, he found himself almost breathless with shock at the realisation that far from being manipulated he was being invited freely to act. It was rather like a story indeed, where the narrative circumstances excitedly followed his own adept imaginings. To think a story, and have it happen! And all of it as naturally consequential upon the leaning forward of Ahraz's slightly parted mouth and its gently touching his own as the fall of a rose-petal might be in high summer when a bee comes blundering for nectar. A kiss is always the opening of a story, and its welcomed narrative leads impetuously onwards in the direction that the story always takes.

Within the silken cube of his bed, no longer alone, Blom now recognised the meaning of the poet's lines:

'The mouth is a guarded gate. The hinges
    open slowly.
The tongue is a prince of pleasure, riding out
    to parley.

He needs no licence to hunt. The field is his.
Battle is declared, and nothing at all is
    forbidden.

The hounds of desire at his side run panting
  and baying.
The sky is darkened with arrows and
  warnings.

Within the forest and willing terror of
  darkness
Bright hoofs of his quarry batter the racing
  ground.

The watchman is too late. The battlements
  are down.
In groans of welcome, gates give way in a
  swoon.

Domes and cupolas, fountains of milk and
  honey,
Acres of spice, jar after jar unspilling.

All is now unlocked to the living tongue
In lavish surrender and yields to
  investigation.

Oh, have you been cradled in the arms of the
  East?
Drowsily nuzzling with the lips? Victory is
  forgiveness.

A Tale

It wells up in you as an underground stream
  rises unseen,
Cave upon cave, beneath the sleeping
  mountains of the night.

Touch, smell and taste are all that are needed
To find the root that reaches to the mother

Where at last we come to her first darkness
And all our restless memory has nothing to
  remember.'

All that he had ever read did not seem as important
as this did now, but he had not previously understood
the poet's images of hunting because he was not a
hunter. And he did not think that the poet fully
acknowledged the general circumstances of encoun-
ters of this kind, where the story is begun, but also
ends. It seemed of a nature not to end, or to end in
metamorphosis or revelation, but for him it ended
too soon. He knew, as the impatient Shahryar knew,
that the story must always come to an end, but should
it end almost as soon as it had begun?

He looked at Ahraz's brown skin laced with the
clear milk of his self-conscious ecstasy, and almost
felt ashamed, as though he had himself become

Shahryar and in an insurmountable fit of violence actually succeeded in preventing Shahrazad from continuing her account of the world.

It was as though he had not been listening to her body.

But Ahraz was smiling, and the smile humbled all pride or shame, just as in her dance she had humbled Razaman. And Blom, in the dutiful consideration that belonged to the character of dullness, left the bed for a ewer of water, a cloth and a bowl of figs. On his return he washed Ahraz, looking carefully for all the places that needed his attention, even under her chin. Then he offered her the figs, and turned away to wash himself.

They lay for a time, occasionally talking of any-thing that it might seem natural to talk about, which was not much. Ahraz was drowsy, for she had tired herself in her dance. She turned her face to the pillows, chewing a fig, and as she crunched the fig-seeds her cheek and temple thundered with the reverberating sound.

'I might be a god containing galaxies,' she thought. And perhaps gods were indeed as careless of their vast creation as men were with their seed. Or were there devouring gods as there were creating gods? In any case (she further considered) it was an essential article of her instructions that Blom's seed was by no means allowed to reach the rich soil that was its natural goal, and there would be many occasions when in order, as it were, to head it off she would be obliged to devour it. But she did not think that such a business gave her the attributes of a god. It would, she thought, make her feel like a slave.

At that timeless moment when they both wandered the shores of sleep, listening to its inviting whisper, which was like the tide that folds and unfolds itself at the bottom of a deep cliff, they were suddenly brought fully awake by a clatter and a shouting that seemed to come from within the room.

Blom thrust his head through the bed-curtains, looking as startled as 'm Baz pretended to be when he gave his puppet-show for the children of the villages, and his puppet-hero surprised the giant in his kitchen. And he was indeed startled, for there had tumbled through the window into his room a half-naked boy of his own age, whose equally startled face bore a remarkable resemblance to his own.

The two faces stared at each other, as though into a mirror, for that mysterious eternity which an unresolved recognition requires, all possible questions drowned in wonder.

Behind, in the arch of the window, with raised arms like an afreet about to pounce, was one of the French soldiers with a harness in one hand and blood dripping from the other. Blom then looked from the boy to the soldier and the soldier to the boy.

And he knew that this image of himself, breathless, terrified, with some fearful thing done to his chest, something planted there or burrowing into it just as the dwarf had burst out of the buffalo, this frail fugitive needed his protection.

25

A WATER clock dripped a late hour, incongruously upon a Louis XIV commode, as though the wedding night had never been disturbed. The palace owl somewhere shrieked a terrified delight at its freedom in hunting, and further away there were sounds of frustrated pursuit and intermittent argument. But the palace guard were usually merry after a feast, and no one paid the sounds much attention.

The three young people had retreated to the bed, seated in a wary but friendly triangulation, with the silken curtains again drawn, as if for the performance of a play to succeed the previous recent private performance there, a conversation piece to provide all possible contrast with the silent but fast-breathing ballet which preceded it, though no one, not even Colonel Marzipol, could have said which was the comedy and which was the melodrama.

It had taken only seconds for Blom to surprise himself and to seize the sword which hung in his chamber with other trophies and playthings of ceremony, and to hold it pointed to the shirt-button of the astonished French orderly, who had not motive or spirit for any sort of struggle. He had brought with him a small trail of blood, a light insistent dropping, which to those who noticed it seemed more likely to have come from the pursued rather than the pursuer. The window was soon barred, and the door too, while the recognition by Ahraz of the neighbouring boy of her childhood (a wonder!) set a seal of perfect safety upon this chance haven for the fugitive of the night.

She saw, indeed, with the sudden piercing clarity which explains dreams or resolves stories, that she had been brought to the palace and to the discipline of a bride as the only means possible of encountering once again the beautiful boy who had been, after all, as she now saw it, her first love. And that Blom, in all his clumsy kindness, was only an excuse, a surrogate, like the player in the Field of the Goat who stands as marker when the goat is first thrown and must wait for his captain to gallop to his position to take it up.

Seeing them now together, she realised what before had only lurked in the margins of her consciousness, that the features of 'l Saqi's boy, framed as she had known them in the concentrating halo of his burnous and so become abstract and iconic, like the visage of a prince on coins, were when framed by the human reality of such appendages as hair and ears, not only more like a boy's, but very much more like Blom's own features. They were both quite reasonably like boys, indeed, but more like each other than anyone else.

But this was only the lesser mystery, for the missing burnous exposed a secret that was much the greater. Not an animal, cradled in kindness, possibly hurt, but a terrible error in nature, concealed in shame, just as we conceal those natural parts which are also nature's imperfections.

Blom, too, confronted what seemed like an answer to a puzzle, for the deformity was revealed not as something inflicted upon the boy (and the orderly with the straps in pursuit with further torture and indignity in mind) but as a strange and familiar element in his very being, perhaps under threat from the French guests, who could say? Was this perhaps what they had come for after all? Would such a thing be a prize in Paris? Was it a legend in the making? Would it be on display to cigar-smoking *flâneurs* at the Café de la Régence?

Blom felt such a threat keenly, all the more since

the visitors were so relaxed, so ingratiating, so insouciant. It was a threat as artful as Colonel Marzipol's gambit out of Philidor, and Blom now thought of that chess master as a boy-devouring monster like the Caliph Razaman, grossly fat, seated upon his divan at the Chess Club and blowing out tobacco smoke through his lifted nostrils, a sort of 'm Baz but with an icy intelligence, a finely tuned and infinitely wicked mind. And Colonel Marzipol was his emissary, his acolyte and procurer, and was insinuating himself with the subtlety of a serpent into the court at Taflat, hoping perhaps that Blom would appoint him Vizier.

The pursued boy was to be protected, therefore, and all that made him unique was to be respected. For the boy spoke soothingly to the stunted legs that grew from his stomach, and caressed the pink uncalloused heels of their feet as though they were the frail bald heads of twin babies nuzzling at his chest.

'Who are you?' Blom had asked, before Ahraz could explain that she knew very well who he was, absorbed in looking into his dark eyes and smiling her recognition so that he should not be afraid, nor see that she for her part was now, despite herself, afraid. But was it fear or was it wonder? Wonder that beauty could live with such a burden, and endure?

Within the racing blood of his own terror, and the taste of the orderly's finger still salt in his mouth like a doubtful delicacy, 'l Isilik stared at his rescuers on the bed. He saw for himself the resemblance of Blom's face to his own, for there had been mirrors enough in 'l Saqi's house. And that the divine Ahraz should be found here was only a momentary surprise, for had he not been brought here himself? Was this place not, after all, the destiny of all young people? A palace of justice, perhaps, where error must be corrected and identities revealed? Perhaps he had now to grow up completely and receive some help in doing so, despite the great effort he had already made himself. There might then come about a correction of errors and the reward of his true role in life, even the uniting of destined spirits, a boy and a girl. From goats and woods to the marvels of the mine, from dust and hunger to the untroubled fountains of the walled garden in Taflat, and now, from the ignominious stench of a basket to the oil-lit shadows and perfumes of a palace: there was, it seemed, an ordained pattern to his life.

But for the time being he could only respond to

Blom's question with the childish mantra of his earliest sense of knowing himself to have become a person, and with the fragments of the villainous cunning he had overheard from his captivity, all run together in a whispered wail that was more a cry for help than an assertion of identity.

'The face with no name,' he said, 'was himself all the same. The Akond will pay, since his first-born lives, and once in the palace, who knows what he'll say? Go back to the wood where your palaces stood: they stand there still. They stand there still.'

Poetry uttered without its sense of occasion turns into madness. Ahraz instinctively put out a calming hand towards him, but her fingers trembled with not knowing what flesh she might touch. The boy shrank back, and for the first time showed defiance.

'Don't touch him!' he cried, loudly this time and with a sudden sharp direct glare that made the hairs on Ahraz's neck stand on end.

'Don't touch him! His name is 'l Isilik, the unknown one! The name with no face took up no space. He has nothing to say to you or to anyone else and he will not be harmed! He would like to go to sleep for ever, but I must be the young Akond!'

Blom could not tell from these wild words if this

was said in deduction or with determination, but he needed some assurance from his bride that the boy must still be a victim and not now a vain impostor.

The orderly had thundered away over the roofs, and the vague sounds of confusion in the palace had by no means died away.

The hoot of the hunting owl came to the ears of in-Blemim as he moved through the cloisters of the palace at a speed consonant with both his dignity and the urgency of his quest. The flowing motion and the flying robes were themselves much like the flight of the owl.

'These night-sounds are an omen of calamity,' he muttered to himself, clutching at his robes to avoid entanglement with the flambeaux attached to the walls, where they might be caught and singed. 'They are identical to the sounds that I heard on the night when Juliba was delivered of the first-born. I feared what they presaged then, and I fear the same tonight, for the boy has survived and has returned, and it is the will of fate, and I must face his claims upon us, and upon the kingdom.'

He had instructed the Wazir to post men in the kitchen yard and around the quarters of the guard and at the postern gates of the palace, but from the vague directions indicated by Captain Debussy's bottle of *aqua dente* it seemed almost certain that the boy had fled over the roofs that led, in a series of dizzying turrets and walk-ways, more or less directly to the private apartments of the palace. In-Blemim had only to ascend at the first opportunity to the highest floor and to hasten along the corridors, entering the apartments and chambers in turn to see if their occupants had been surprised by a nocturnal visitor.

But this took time. In some of the rooms, those who were asleep, or were pretending to be asleep, or who had something to hide, cared nothing for the urgency of the Akond's questions but bowed and smiled and muttered their muddled phrases of court protocol. On his way, the Akond collected his father, who was in the profoundest slumber of all, since his customary wakefulness and anxiety had been quite dispelled by his decision to live for the moment, and if the decision led him easily into a moment's sleep that might go on for ever, so be it, for he had concluded that to wake to another day was as surprising a thing as could happen to him now, and would seem like a new life. The result was that he slept like a baby.

A Tale

And woke like a baby, eager for attention. He would not return to his bed until in-Blemim had explained everything.

26

WHEN explanations are demanded, the explanations that are offered come forward awkwardly, like clumsy lovers uncertain of their charm for each other. But as love itself is a reassurance, so the plain truth is always met with a grateful surmounting of disbelief. The plain truth settles everything.

'So your first-born survived,' said the old Akond, 'and I was a grandfather for a full year without knowing it! By rights that should have shortened my prospects. But since I was in ignorance it cannot have affected me. And in any case I am a changed man, and henceforward will take short views.'

'I am glad to hear it,' said the Akond, 'but we are losing time. The boy is on the roof and may come to harm. I can't allow it, since he is my first-born, despite his deformity, and it was a great error to have had him taken away.'

The old Akond scratched himself beneath his night-gown and pondered. He had always thought his son intolerant of the waywardness of human nature and of things in general.

'We should not struggle unduly against the fates,' he said. 'These Frenchmen have been bad for you. They are Prometheans, and there is no peace in their souls. They would pull the rose to pieces in search of its smell.'

'You are right,' said in-Blemim.

'And if you think that they are chasing your first-born across the roof-tops, perhaps you should have gone that way yourself, and followed them. However, if the boy is pursued and terrified, would he not have sought the first help that he could see? All of us are asleep in this wing of the palace, dreaming of buffalo. Our lamps are dimmed. But come to the window. Look: across there the lamps are still burning, lively with the restless and ever-renewable fires of love! It is the chamber of the young Akond and his bride. Let us make our way there.'

They did so, and had to kick the eunuch awake who was snoring against the door, his scimitar in his lap and an empty flagon rolled to his feet. And inside the room they found Blom and Ahraz and 'l Isilik together, sitting in the tent of the bed like warriors negotiating the peace of hostilities that were never begun in the first place, with no advantages to seek and no grudges to bear, but with every conviction that something had to be resolved.

Who could resolve it? It needed the tradition of an art, whereby the intractable issue could be sung and debated at length, like that of the Camel and the Elephant. Perhaps in future times such a play would be performed, even if it were as little appreciated by its audience as that favourite epic had been enjoyed by Colonel Marzipol. Perhaps Marzipol and his adventurers would themselves appear in it, as foreign demons playing the agents of discovery, demanding the life of the blemished hero as the price of order, knowledge and reason.

In-Blemim knew that it was only custom that was at fault, for he knew that he was not, in the end, a tyrant like the Caliph Razaman. He was not unjust. He put his own interests after the interests of his people. He had been frightened by the deformed baby, and had bowed to the superstitious urgings of the women attendant upon the birth. He had, like any provident man, wished for an heir who was worthy of his finer aspirations. But what he had ordered was wrong. He knew that even a prince could not live free from the whims of nature, and to defy nature was merely to put oneself further in her debt.

Uz-Blemim agreed for once.

'She is a hard mistress of men,' he said. 'But I have learned that we must accept her decrees.'

They were appalled at the sport that nature had played with the first-born's body, for what in a baby looks like an agglomeration of organic error hard to disentangle, unbearable to look upon, and unlikely in any case to survive, in a boy of fifteen becomes the history of a long-suffering survival against the odds. To see him huddled with his brother and his brother's bride, they themselves so touching in their innocent acceptance of the strange customs of the country, brought a flood of helpless tenderness to the Akonds' gaze, like an unsuspected seepage in a dam that reveals not a fault of engineering design but the natural and wholly beneficent force of the water that it has been hoarding.

'The boy is not long for this world,' said uz-Blemim. 'He has been starved, and perhaps already cut, and the parasite drains his energy. But it is well that we take him in, for the palace is more than a haven to him. It is his rightful home.'

'You are right again,' said in-Blemim. 'How good

it is to have you here at last with me. In Samira we had our differences, but here we think as one.'

They ordered food for the first-born, who had already devoured the remaining nuptial sweetmeats offered him by Blom and Ahraz, and they again kicked the eunuch awake into duty.

'Go into the women's quarters,' said in-Blemim, 'and fetch your mistress Juliba, and also uz-Mabmabla, for it is right that they should now receive their lost son and grandson.'

The eunuch lumbered away into the darkness.

It is not to be supposed that Juliba was ignorant in the matter of her first-born. Although it may have suited the Akond to believe otherwise, a woman cannot give birth among the faithful attendants of her own sex without some hints and intuitions of the outcome, however much it needed to be hidden. A confinement within a place of such particular confinement may breed secrets, but in the breeding of them they germinate and spread. Dark words and gossip, whispers and commiserations, chance allusions and unforced memories had completed the troublingly incomplete narrative in her mind. Officially, the child had died, and in-Blemim did not like to speak of it, but Juliba knew what she knew, and uz-Mabmabla knew more.

Faced with 'l Isilik, a dark-eyed waif soiling the silken sheets of the bridal bed and clutching to his chest an unspeakable horror which she could barely look upon twice, Juliba felt her heart give a great leap as if it were a climber venturing too far upon the edge of a cliff. She was brought back, as if for safety, to the hopes and vistas of her youth and first prospective motherhood, and knew once more that it was an eminence too great for any woman not to be fraught with danger. The danger was now all before her, and the regret for time passed, and the choking assault upon her of an unnegotiated love.

In the privacy of their apartments, princes may weep and embrace, even though those who attend them or write up the annals of the kingdom may not speak of it.

They were conscious, all of them, of their gathering together in a finality that might also be a beginning, a scene of summary resolve in which, though nothing could be uttered, there was everything to be said. Thoughts were loud as actors competing to soliloquise, bodies motionless as in a painting of witness and justice.

Uz-Mabmabla said: 'The palace owl has finished

his punishing cries for the night, but this does not mean that death is defeated, merely postponed.'

And uz-Blemim said: 'Those who may not live long, whether they are old or young, must rejoice in what they have. Dawn is quietly visible beyond the turrets and the solomon trees once again achieve their knotty profiles. Today is a new day, and already in inexorable motion towards who knows what end, but yesterday at least I was immortal.'

And in-Blemim said: 'The decrees of a prince must be seen to achieve a parallel harmony like an opening in chess. As I have welcomed my father back to the palace, so I must welcome back my first-born. As I have exiled Anic to the governance of the spice fields, so I must send Colonel Marzipol away, for his influence, too, is unbalancing. Too much cold reason is as fatal as a superfluity of passion. Let the French party cross the Indus as they intended, and attempt to impress the British in their stronghold of tea and cotton. Is that likely? I think not.'

And Juliba said: 'Every man possesses an angel spirit who longs in fiery emptiness for a human body. Sometimes the angel enters him at a time of crisis, as the hero Medona was infused by the angelic power that enabled him to defeat Razaman. But in the case of princes, their angels are so eager to be embodied that they imperiously plunge through the stars and clouds so that they may enter them at the moment of their conception, a dazzling dive through the firmament, a million leagues towards an inconsiderable target, a comet stalking a seed. Who can blame them if they fail? For without his angel a man would be a poor creature indeed, living the life of a sheep. My first-born's angel tried, and missed by an inch. If he dies, it will be his angel pulling him back to the heavens, like a hooked fish. The boy is terrible to look upon, but more terrible is a mother's connivance in rejecting a child, and most terrible of all is every mother's knowledge that all her children will eventually die.'

And Blom said: 'So, he is my brother.'

And 'l Isilik said: 'And *he* is also your brother.'

And Ahraz said: 'They are like flowers on a single stem, though you may not trim them for the vase. A prince, too, is unique, just as there is only one way to cut a precious stone. His brother may be a betrayer, but equally may also need protection. Our destiny is only one version of our dreams, when the face that we find is a copy of the face that we imagined, and the human seam is infinite and may be considered rubies.'

And the fifth Akond said nothing, for he was nothing but a flaw buried in blood, tormenting the eye with his sad fragments of human shape.

As the sun grew stronger and the servants knew no better than to busy themselves noisily as usual in the deeper parts of the palace, the morning declared itself arrived at last. Ahraz took Blom and 'l Isilik, one in each hand, and descended into the courtyard, where the fountains had already begun to assemble their momentary contraptions. An arm drawn through the tumbling water and across the brow refreshed them and put sleeplessness behind them as they walked towards 'm Baz's stage that still stood at one side. The tambours of the musicians were lying silently upon it, and the blossoms and crimson streamers of the court conjuror turned slightly in a morning breeze that also animated the vines that curled upwards to the ironwork balconies, now empty of spectators, and stirred the linen flaps of the great shell from which Ahraz had last night triumphantly emerged. The pace of day was as slow and tentative as the night's dance had been decisive, dividing as it did the heroic past from the uncertain future, the known from the unknown, the learned from the extemporised, the achieved story from the uncompleted world that it described. The trio walked together in their youth and exhaustion, neither happy nor unhappy, confident of nothing in particular, accepting things as the young are required to do.

The painted shell was still there, looking in the strengthening sunlight exactly what it was intended to be, an artifice designed to make things appear, or perhaps to disappear.

After a moment, not so much of hesitation as of a kind of recognition, still holding hands, they went inside.

www.randomhouse.co.uk/vintage